THE WORLD OF
ASTRID LINDGREN

PiPPi
LONGSTOCKING

OXFORD
UNIVERSITY PRESS

Great Clarendon Street, Oxford OX2 6DP
Oxford University Press is a department of the University of Oxford.
It furthers the University's objective of excellence in research, scholarship,
and education by publishing worldwide. Oxford is a registered trade mark of
Oxford University Press in the UK and in certain other countries

First published in 1945 by Rabén & Sjögren, Sweden as *Pippi Långstrump*.
For more information about Astrid Lindgren, see www.astridlindgren.com.
All foreign rights are handled by The Astrid Lindgren Company, Lidingö, Sweden.
For more information, please contact info@astridlindgren.se

Pictures by Mini Grey
Translated by Susan Beard

The moral rights of the author have been asserted

Database right Oxford University Press (maker)

First published 1945
This edition 2020

British Library Cataloguing in Publication Data

Data available

ISBN: 978-0-19-277631-0

3 5 7 9 10 8 6 4 2

Printed in India by Manipal Technologies Limited

Paper used in the production of this book is a natural,
recyclable product made from wood grown in sustainable forests.
The manufacturing process conforms to the environmental
regulations of the country of origin.

Pippi
LONGSTOCKING

BY ASTRID LINDGREN
ILLUSTRATED BY MINI GREY
TRANSLATED BY SUSAN BEARD

OXFORD
UNIVERSITY PRESS

CONTENTS

PIPPI MOVES INTO VILLA VILLEKULLA

On the edge of the tiny little town was an old garden, all overgrown. In this garden was an old house and in that house lived Pippi Longstocking. She was nine years old and she lived there all alone. She didn't have a mum or a dad, and that was actually quite nice because there was nobody to tell her to go to bed just when she was having the most fun, and nobody to make her take cod liver oil when she would rather eat sweets.

Pippi had a dad once, and she'd liked him ever so much—she had a mum too, of course, but that was such a long time ago she couldn't remember anything about it. Her mum had died when Pippi was a tiny, tiny baby who lay in her cot and screamed and screamed so horrendously that no one could go near her. Pippi thought her mum

1

was up in heaven looking down on her little girl through a peephole, and Pippi often waved to her up there and said:

'Don't worry! I'll be all right!'

Pippi hadn't forgotten her dad. He was a ship's captain and sailed the great oceans, and Pippi had sailed with him until the time he blew overboard in a huge storm and disappeared. But Pippi was absolutely certain he would come back one day. She didn't believe he had drowned at all. She thought he had washed ashore on an island in the South Seas and become the island king, and was walking around all day with a golden crown on his head.

'My mum is an angel and my dad is a South Sea Island king. Not every child has such special parents, you know,' Pippi always said, sounding pleased with herself. 'And as soon as my dad can build a boat he'll come and fetch me and then I'll be a South Sea Island princess. What a time we'll have, tra-la-la!'

Many years ago her dad had bought the old house that stood in the garden. He had planned to live there with Pippi when he got too old and doddery to sail the oceans any longer. But then, of course, that annoying thing happened, when he was blown into the sea, so while she was waiting for him to come back Pippi went straight home to Villa Villekulla. That was the name of the house. It stood there, ready and waiting, with furniture and everything. One beautiful summer's evening she said goodbye to all the shipmates on her dad's boat. They were so fond of Pippi, and Pippi was fond of them.

'Cheerio, lads,' Pippi said, giving each and every one a kiss on the forehead. 'Don't worry about me. I'll be all right!'

She took two things with her from the boat. A little monkey called Mr Nilsson—a present from her dad—and a big travel bag full of golden coins. The shipmates stood on the deck and watched Pippi walk away until they couldn't see her any more. She strode on with Mr Nilsson on her shoulder and the travel bag in her hand, and didn't look round once.

'A remarkable child,' said one of the shipmates, wiping a tear from his eye as Pippi disappeared into the distance.

He was right. Pippi was a very remarkable child. And the most remarkable thing about her was her strength. She was so spectacularly strong that in the whole wide world there was no one as strong as she was, not even a policeman. She could lift up a whole horse if she wanted to. And she did want to. She had her own horse that she had bought with one of her gold coins the very same day she came home to Villa Villekulla. She had always longed for a horse of her own and now she had one, and he lived on the veranda. But when it was time for Pippi's afternoon coffee she picked him up and put him in the garden with no problem at all.

Next to Villa Villekulla there was another garden and another house. In that house lived a dad and a mum with their two sweet little children, a boy and a girl. The boy was called Tommy and the girl was called Annika.

They were two very polite and well-behaved and obedient children. Tommy never bit his nails and he always did as his mum told him. Annika never argued when she couldn't have her own way, and she was always very neat in her well-ironed cotton dresses, which she was careful not to get dirty. Tommy and Annika played very nicely together in their garden but they often wished for a friend to play with, and while Pippi was still sailing around on the ocean with her dad they used to hang over the fence and say to each other:

'It's stupid that no one ever moves into that house! Someone should be living there. Someone with children.'

On that beautiful summer's evening when Pippi walked through the door of Villa Villekulla for the first time, Tommy and Annika weren't at home. They had gone to stay with their grandma for a week. That's why they had no idea that someone had moved in next door. And the day after they came home and were standing at their gate, looking into the street, they still didn't know that there actually was someone to play with so close by. Just as they were standing there, wondering what to do, and whether anything interesting was going to happen that day or whether it was going to be one of those boring days when there was nothing to do— just then the gate of Villa Villekulla opened and a little girl walked out. She was the strangest little girl Tommy and Annika had ever seen. It was Pippi Longstocking, going for her morning stroll. This is what she looked like:

Her hair was the same colour as a carrot and was in two tights plaits that stuck straight out. Her nose looked exactly like a small potato and was smothered in freckles. Under her nose was an extraordinarily wide mouth full of healthy white teeth. Her dress was quite peculiar. Pippi had sewn it herself. It was supposed to be blue but the blue material had run out, so Pippi had to put red patches here and there. On her long, thin legs she wore a pair of long stockings, one brown and the other black, and she was also wearing a pair of black shoes that were precisely twice as long as her feet. Pippi's dad had bought them for her in South America, big enough for her to grow into, and Pippi wouldn't wear anything else.

What especially amazed Tommy and Annika was the monkey sitting on the new girl's shoulder. It was a little squirrel monkey, dressed in blue trousers, a yellow jacket and a white straw hat.

Pippi set off down the street. She walked with one foot on the pavement and the other in the gutter. Tommy and Annika stared after her until they couldn't see her any more. After a while she came back, and this time she was walking backwards. That was so she didn't have to turn round to walk home. When she reached Tommy and Annika's gate she stopped. The children looked at each other in silence. At last Tommy said:

'Why did you walk backwards?'

'Why I walked backwards?' Pippi said. 'We live in a free country, don't we? Aren't you allowed to walk any way you want? Let me tell you that in Egypt every single person walks like that and no one thinks it's strange in the slightest.'

'How do you know?' asked Tommy. 'You've never been to Egypt.'

'Me, not been to Egypt! That's news to me. I've been everywhere in the entire world and seen much stranger things than people walking backwards. I wonder what you'd have said if I'd walked on my hands like they do in Furthest India?'

'Now you're lying,' Tommy said.

Pippi thought about that for a moment.

'Yes, you're right. I am lying,' she said sadly.

'It's bad to tell lies,' said Annika, who had at last dared to open her mouth.

'Yes, it's *very* bad to tell lies,' said Pippi, even more sadly. 'But you see, I forget from time to time. And how can anyone expect a little child who has an angel for a mum and a South Sea Island king for a dad, and who has sailed around on the sea the whole of her life, to tell the truth all the time? And by the way,' she added, the whole of her freckly face beaming, 'let me tell you that in the Congo not one single person tells the truth. They lie all day. They start at seven in the morning and carry on until the sun goes down. So if I happen to lie now and then you'll have to try and forgive me, and remember it's because I lived in the Congo for too long. But we can still be friends, can't we?'

'Of course,' said Tommy, and he suddenly felt that this was probably not going to be one of those boring days.

'By the way, why not come and eat breakfast with me?' Pippi asked.

'Since you're asking,' said Tommy, 'why not? Come on, let's go!'

'Yes,' said Annika. 'Right now!'

'But first I must introduce you to Mr Nilsson,' Pippi said. The little monkey took off his hat and bowed politely.

So they walked through Villa Villekulla's garden gate, which was falling to pieces, and up the gravel path lined with ancient trees covered in moss—perfect climbing trees by the look of them—to the house and onto the veranda. There stood the horse, chomping oats from a soup tureen.

'Why on earth have you got a horse on the veranda?' asked Tommy. All the horses he knew lived in a stable.

'Well,' said Pippi, thinking. 'He'd only be in the way in the kitchen. And he doesn't like the sitting room.'

Tommy and Annika patted the horse and then they carried on into the house. Inside there was a kitchen, a sitting room and a bedroom, but it looked as if Pippi had forgotten to do the weekly cleaning. Tommy and Annika looked around nervously in case that South Sea Island king was sitting in a corner. They had never seen a South Sea Island king in all their life. But there was no dad, and no mum either, and Annika asked anxiously:

'Do you live here all alone?'

'Definitely not,' said Pippi. 'Mr Nilsson and the horse live here too.'

'No, I mean, haven't you got a mum or a dad here?'

'No, not at all,' said Pippi cheerfully.

'But who tells you when it's time to go to bed every evening, and that kind of thing?' Annika asked.

'I do that myself,' said Pippi. 'First I tell myself once, very nicely, and if I don't obey I tell myself again, quite crossly, and if I still don't obey, well, then there's trouble, I can tell you.'

Tommy and Annika didn't really understand this but thought it might be a good way to go about it. By this time they had reached the kitchen and all of a sudden Pippi yelled:

'Mixy-mixy, pancake-ixy
Bakey-bakey, pancake-makey
Take your seaty, pancake-eaty'

She took out three eggs and threw them high into the air. One dropped on her head and broke, and the egg yolk dripped into her eyes. But she expertly caught the others in a saucepan where they cracked open.

'Well, they say egg yolk is good for your hair,' Pippi said, wiping her eyes. 'You watch, it'll come sprouting out of my head now. In Brazil, by the way, everyone walks around with egg in their hair, and of course you never see a bald head anywhere. There was only one man silly enough to eat up all his eggs instead of putting them on his head. And do you know what? He went bald, as expected. And whenever he set foot outside there was such a hullabaloo the police had to be called for.'

While she had been speaking Pippi had very handily scooped all the pieces of egg shell out of the saucepan with her fingers. Then she took a long-handled scrubbing brush from its hook on the wall and began whisking the pancake batter so fast it splashed all over the walls. Finally she poured what was left into a pancake pan that was heating on the stove. When the pancake was cooked on one side she tossed it half-way to the ceiling and caught it in the pan again, and when it was ready she threw it right across the kitchen and onto a plate that was waiting on the table.

'Eat!' she shouted. 'Eat, before it gets cold!'

Tommy and Annika ate and thought it was a very delicious pancake. Afterwards Pippi invited them into the sitting room. There was only one piece of furniture in there. It was an enormous writing bureau with lots and lots of small drawers. Pippi opened the drawers and showed Tommy and Annika all the treasures she kept inside. There were fantastic birds' eggs and odd-looking shells and stones, pretty little boxes, beautiful silver mirrors, and strings of beads, and all sorts of other things that Pippi and her dad had bought on their travels round the world. Pippi gave her new friends a present each, so they would always remember the day. Tommy got a dagger with a shimmering mother-of-pearl handle, and Annika a small box with a lid covered in pink shells. Inside the box lay a ring with a green stone.

'Why not go home now, so you can come back again tomorrow?' said Pippi. 'Because unless you go home, you can't come back, you see. And that would be a pity.'

Annika and Tommy agreed, and so they went home, past the horse that had eaten up all the oats, and through Villa Villekulla's garden gate. Mr Nilsson waved his hat as they left.

PIPPI IS A THING-FINDER AND GETS INTO A FIGHT

Annika woke up early next morning. She leapt out of bed and padded over to Tommy.

'Wake up, Tommy,' she said, pulling his arm. 'Wake up so we can go to that funny girl with the big shoes!'

Suddenly Tommy was wide awake.

'I knew when I was asleep that today would be fun, but I couldn't remember why,' he said, struggling out of his pyjama jacket. Then off they both dashed to the bathroom where they brushed their teeth and washed much faster than usual. Their clothes flew on in double-quick time, and a whole hour before their mother was expecting them they came sliding down the bannister and

14

landed at the breakfast table, where they called out for their hot chocolate to be served *immediately*.

'What's going on?' their mother asked. 'Seeing as you're in such a hurry.'

'We're going to see the new girl who's moved in next door,' said Tommy.

'We might be gone all day,' said Annika.

♥

That morning Pippi was in the middle of baking ginger biscuits. She had made a huge ball of dough and was rolling it out on the kitchen floor.

'And I'll tell you why,' she said to her little monkey. 'What good is a table top when you've got to make at least five hundred ginger biscuits?'

There she was, kneeling on the floor and cutting out biscuits at lightning speed.

'Stop treading in the dough, Mr Nilsson,' she snapped, just as the doorbell rang.

Pippi ran and opened it. She was as white as a miller from head to toe, and when she energetically shook hands with Annika and Tommy they were drenched in a cloud of flour.

'How very nice of you to look in,' she said, shaking her apron and sending up another cloud of flour. Tommy and Annika got so much flour in their mouths it made them cough.

'What are you doing?' asked Tommy.

'Well, I could tell you I'm cleaning the chimney, but you're far too smart to believe that,' said Pippi. 'In actual fact, I'm baking. But I'll be finished in a jiffy. You can sit on the log box and wait.'

She could certainly work fast, that girl! Tommy and Annika sat on the log box and watched her stamp out biscuit shapes all over the dough, hurl them onto the baking trays and then throw the trays into the oven. It was almost like watching a film, they thought.

'Done!' Pippi said finally, taking out the last tray and slamming the oven door shut with a bang.

'What shall we do now?' Tommy asked.

'I don't know what you're thinking of doing,' Pippi said. 'But I'm not the kind to put my feet up. I am, in fact, a thing-finder, and thing-finders never get a minute's rest.'

'What did you say you were?' asked Annika.

'A thing-finder.'

'What's that?' asked Tommy.

'Someone who finds things, of course! What else could it be?' said Pippi, as she swept all the flour on the floor into a small pile. 'The whole world is full of things and there's a crying need for someone to find them. And that's just what a thing-finder does.'

'What kind of things?' asked Annika.

'Oh, all sorts,' said Pippi. 'Clumps of gold, ostrich feathers, dead rats, teeny-weeny nuts and bolts. Stuff like that.'

Tommy and Annika thought it sounded good fun and they really wanted to be thing-finders too. Although Tommy said he'd rather find a clump of gold than a dead rat.

'We'll have to see what turns up,' said Pippi. 'Something always does. But let's get a move on in case any other thing-finders come along and make off with all the clumps of gold around here.'

The three thing-finders set off. They thought it was best to start looking among the houses close by, because Pippi said that even if it was perfectly possible to find a little nail or bolt in the middle of a forest, the best things were actually found close to where people lived.

'But on the other hand,' she said. 'I have seen examples of quite the opposite. I remember the time I was looking for things in the jungles of Borneo. Right in the very middle of the rainforest, where no one had ever set foot before, what do you think I found? I'll tell you: a very fine wooden leg. I gave it away later to an old man with only one leg, and he said you couldn't buy such a fine wooden leg even if you had heaps of money.'

Tommy and Annika watched Pippi closely to see how a thing-finder behaved. Pippi ran from one side of the road to the other, shaded her eyes with her hand, and looked and looked. Sometimes she crawled on her knees, stuck her hand through fences and said disappointedly:

'Odd! I was absolutely *sure* I saw a clump of gold.'

'Can we really take everything we find?' asked Annika.

'Yes, everything that's lying on the ground,' said Pippi.

Further down the road an elderly gent was sleeping on the lawn outside his house.

'He's lying on the ground,' Pippi said. 'And we've found him. Let's have 'im!'

Tommy and Annika were flabbergasted.

'No, no, Pippi, we can't take an old man, we just

can't,' said Tommy. 'What do we want him for, anyway?'

'What do we want him for? We could use him for lots of things. We could put him in a little rabbit hutch instead of a rabbit and feed him dandelion leaves. But if you'd rather not, well, that's fine by me. But it really annoys me to think another thing-finder might come along and pinch him.'

They walked on. All of a sudden Pippi gave an ear-splitting yell.

'Oh, I've never seen anything like this!' she shouted, picking up a rusty old tin from the grass. 'What a find! What a *find*! You can never have too many tins.'

Tommy looked at the tin doubtfully and said:

'What can you use *that* for?'

'Oh, you can use it for lots of things,' Pippi said. 'You could put biscuits in it, for one thing. Then it would be one of those nice Tins For Biscuits. On the other hand, you don't *have* to put biscuits in it, and then it will be one of those Tins Not For Biscuits. It's not quite so nice, mind you, but that's all right too.'

She studied the tin, which really was very rusty indeed and also had a hole in the bottom.

'This almost looks as if it's a Tin Not For Biscuits,' she said thoughtfully. 'But you can always plonk it over your head and pretend it's the middle of the night.'

So she did. With the tin over her head she walked along like a little metal tower and didn't stop until she fell over a fence and onto her stomach. There was a loud crash as the tin hit the ground.

'There, you see,' said Pippi, taking off the tin. 'If I hadn't had that on my head I would have fallen flat on my face and bashed myself stupid.'

'But,' said Annika, 'if you hadn't had the tin on your head you wouldn't have tripped over the fence in the first place.'

Just as Annika finished speaking Pippi gave another yelp and triumphantly held up an empty cotton reel.

'It must be my lucky day today,' she said. 'Such a dear, sweet little cotton reel to blow bubbles with or hang on a piece of string and have as a necklace! I want to go home and do it this very minute.'

At that moment one of the garden gates opened and a boy came racing out. He looked scared and that wasn't surprising, because hot on his heels came five boys. They soon caught up with him and shoved him up against a fence where they all started piling into him. All five at once began hitting and punching him. He was crying and holding up his arms to protect his face.

'Get 'im, boys,' shouted the biggest and strongest boy. 'He'll never dare show his face on this street again!'

'Oh,' said Annika. 'That's Viktor they're beating up. How can they be so mean!'

'It's that nasty Bengt. He's always fighting,' said Tommy. 'Five against one as well. The cowards!'

Pippi walked over to the boys and prodded Bengt in the back.

'Sorry to bother you,' she said. 'But are you planning to make minced meat of little Viktor, seeing as five of you are having a go at him at once?'

Bengt turned round to see a girl he had never met before. A completely unknown girl, daring to prod him in the back. At first he gaped in utter astonishment, and then a wide smile spread across his face.

'Boys,' he said. 'Boys! Leave Viktor and come and have a look at this little girlie. Oh ho, what a girlie!'

He slapped his knees and laughed. In a flash they had all gathered around Pippi—all except Viktor, that is, who wiped his tears and cautiously went to stand next to Tommy.

'Have you ever seen such hair? It's like a bonfire! And those shoes!' Bengt continued. 'Can I borrow one of them? I want to go out rowing but I haven't got a boat.'

Then he took hold of one of Pippi's plaits but dropped it immediately, saying:

'Ouch, I burned myself!'

Then all five boys stood in a circle around Pippi and leapt up and down, shouting:

'Red Riding Hood, Red Riding Hood!'

Pippi stood in the middle of the circle, smiling in a friendly way. Bengt hoped she would cry or get angry. She should be looking scared by now, at the very least. When nothing he did worked, he gave her a shove.

'I don't think you have an especially charming

way with the ladies,' said Pippi. And with that she lifted him high in the air on her strong arms, carried him over to a birch tree that was growing nearby, and hung him over a branch. Then she took the next boy and hung him over a different branch. She sat the next one up on a tall gatepost outside one of the houses, and threw the next boy right over a fence so that he landed in the middle of the flowerbed in a front garden. Then she sat the last one in a child's wheelbarrow that had been left in the road. Pippi, Tommy, Annika, and Viktor stood looking at the boys, who were stunned into silence. Then Pippi said:

'You're bullies! Five of you, attacking one boy. That's cowardly. And then you start pushing a defenceless little girl about. Naughty, naughty!'

'Come on, let's go home,' she said to Tommy and Annika. And then she said to Viktor:

'If they try to beat you up again, just tell me.'

Bengt was sitting up in the tree, not daring to move a muscle. Pippi said to him:

'If there's anything else you'd like to say about my hair or my shoes then you'd better say it now before I go home.'

But Bengt didn't have anything else to say

about Pippi's shoes, or her hair either. So with her rusty tin in one hand and her cotton reel in the other, Pippi walked away, followed by Tommy and Annika.

When they reached Pippi's garden she said:

'Oh, my goodness, how annoying! Here's me, with two lovely things I've found, and you haven't got anything. You must carry on searching. Tommy, why don't you take a look in that old tree? Old trees are one of the very best places for a thing-finder to look.'

Tommy said he didn't think he and Annika would ever find anything at all, but to please Pippi he stuck his hand into a hollow in the tree trunk.

'What?' he said, absolutely astonished, and pulled out his hand. He was holding a brilliant little notebook with a leather cover, and it had a small silver pen in a special holder.

'That was pretty strange,' said Tommy.

'There, you see? There's nothing better than being a thing-finder. It's very odd that more people don't want the job. They can be carpenters and shoemakers and chimney sweeps and so on, but never a thing-finder. Oh no, that's not good enough for them!'

And then she said to Annika:

'Why don't you feel inside that old tree stump? You find things in tree stumps practically all the time.'

Annika pushed in her hand and almost straight away found a red coral necklace. She and Tommy stood gaping for ages, they were so amazed. And then they thought that from now on they would be thing-finders every day.

Pippi had been up half the night practising ball-throwing and she suddenly felt very sleepy.

'I think I need a little snooze,' she said. 'Can you come with me and tuck me in?'

As Pippi sat on the edge of her bed and took off her shoes, she looked at them thoughtfully and said:

'So he was going rowing, was he, that Bengt? Huh!' She snorted scornfully, 'I'll teach him to row all right! Next time!'

'Tell me, Pippi,' Tommy said, respectfully. 'Why have you got such big shoes?'

'So I can waggle my toes, of course,' she replied. Then she lay down to sleep. She always slept with her feet on the pillow and her head underneath the covers.

'This is how they sleep in Guatemala,' she declared. 'It really is the only way to sleep. And it also means I can waggle my toes while I'm asleep.'

'Can you sleep without a lullaby?' she went on. 'I always have to sing to myself for a little while, otherwise I don't get a wink of sleep.'

Tommy and Annika could hear mumbling coming from under the covers. It was Pippi, singing herself to sleep. Very quietly they tip-toed out, so as not to disturb her. In the doorway they turned round and looked back at the bed. All they could see was Pippi's feet on the pillow. There she lay, waggling her toes up and down.

♥

Tommy and Annika scooted off home. Annika held her coral necklace tight in her hand.

'It seems a little bit odd,' she said. 'Tommy, you don't think . . . you don't think Pippi put those things there first?'

'You never know,' said Tommy. 'You never know anything as far as Pippi's concerned.'

PIPPI PLAYS TAG
WITH THE POLICE

Everyone in the town soon knew that a little girl of nine years old was living alone in Villa Villekulla. And the grown-ups thought that wouldn't do at all. Children needed someone to give them a good talking to, and children had to go to school and learn their multiplication tables. So that is why all the grown-ups of the town decided that the little girl in Villa Villekulla must be sent to a children's home without delay.

One beautiful afternoon Pippi invited Tommy and Annika over for coffee and ginger biscuits. She served the coffee on the veranda steps. It was warm and sunny there, and the air was filled with the scent of the flowers in Pippi's garden. Mr Nilsson climbed up and down the veranda railing, and now and then the horse stuck his nose in for a ginger biscuit.

'This is the life,' Pippi said, stretching out her legs as far as they would go.

Just then two policemen in full uniform came in through the gate.

'Aha,' said Pippi. 'This must be my lucky day. I like policemen more than anything. After rhubarb crumble.'

And she walked towards the policemen with a big beaming smile on her face.

'Could this be the girl who's moved into Villa Villekulla?' asked one of the policemen.

'Wrong!' said Pippi. 'This is a very little auntie who lives on the third floor on the other side of town.'

She said that only because she wanted to joke with the policemen, but they didn't think it was funny at all. They said she shouldn't try to be clever. And then they told her that all the kind people of the town had found room for her in a children's home.

'I've already got room in a children's home,' Pippi said.

'What's that?' said one of the policemen. 'Which children's home?'

'This one,' said Pippi. 'I'm a child and this is my home. So, this is a children's home. And I've got room here, lots of room.'

'My dear child,' said the policeman, smiling. 'You don't quite understand. You've got to move to a proper children's home and have someone look after you.'

'Do they let you have horses at that children's home?' Pippi asked.

'No, certainly not,' said the policeman.

'I thought as much,' said Pippi. 'Monkeys, then?'

'Well, of course not.'

'I see,' said Pippi. 'Then you'll have to get kids for your children's home from somewhere else. I'm not going there.'

'But surely you understand that you must go to school?' said the policeman.

'Why must I go to school?'

'To learn things, of course.'

'What kind of things?'

'All sorts,' said the policeman. 'Lots of useful things, like multiplication tables, for a start.'

'I've managed very well without multi-kipperation tables for the past nine years,' said Pippi. 'And I expect I'll go on managing in the future.'

'Yes, but think how sad it will make you, being so ignorant. Imagine when you're a grown-up and someone asks you what the capital city of Portugal is, and you can't answer.'

'I certainly can answer,' said Pippi. 'I can answer like this: if you are so desperately keen to find out what the capital city of Portugal is, why not write to Portugal and ask?'

'But wouldn't you think it was a pity that you didn't know?'

'Quite possibly,' said Pippi. 'I expect I'll lie awake at night wondering and wondering: darn it, what is the capital city of Portugal? But you can't have fun all the time,' Pippi continued, and stood on her head. 'By the way, I've been to Lisbon with my dad,' she said, from upside down, because she could talk that way up, too.

But then one of the policemen said Pippi shouldn't believe she could do exactly as she jolly well pleased. She would have to go with them to the children's home, pronto. He walked up to her and grabbed her arm. But Pippi quickly broke free, gave him a gentle pat and said: 'Tag!' And before he could blink she had hopped onto the veranda railing. In two seconds she scrambled up onto the balcony above the veranda. The policemen weren't keen on climbing up the same way, which is why they charged into the house and up the stairs. But by the time they got to the balcony, Pippi was already halfway up the roof. She was climbing over the roof tiles just as if she was a monkey. In a flash she was up on the ridge and jumped conveniently onto the chimney pot. Down on the balcony stood the two policemen, scratching their heads, and on the lawn stood Tommy and Annika, staring up at Pippi.

'What *fun* it is, playing tag!' shouted Pippi. 'It was *so* kind of you to visit. And it really is my lucky day, that's plain to see.'

After the policemen had thought for a while they went and found a ladder, which they propped against the house wall. And they climbed up, one behind the other, to bring Pippi down. But they looked rather nervous as they stepped onto the ridge of the roof and began wobbling towards Pippi.

'Don't be afraid,' called Pippi. 'It's not dangerous. It's fun!'

When the policemen were only two steps away from Pippi she jumped down from the chimney and scampered to the other end of the roof, laughing and shouting. A few metres away from the house stood a tree.

'Watch me dive!' Pippi cried, and she leapt down into the leafy treetop and hung onto a branch for a while, swinging backwards and forwards, before dropping to the ground. Then she shot off to the other end of the house and took away the ladder.

The policemen had looked rather startled when Pippi jumped, but they became even more startled when they clambered along the roof to the other end and tried to get down. At first they were absolutely furious and shouted to Pippi, who was standing on the ground below looking up at them, that she must put the ladder back instantly, otherwise there would be trouble.

'Why are you so angry?' Pippi scolded them. 'We're only playing tag, so we should be friends!'

The policemen thought about that, and eventually one of them said meekly:

'Er, um, would you be kind enough to put the ladder back so we can come down?'

'Goes without saying,' said Pippi, and straight away she propped the ladder against the wall again. 'And then we can all have coffee together and have a lovely time.'

But the policemen were only being cunning, because as soon as they were down on the ground they rushed at Pippi, saying:

'We'll teach you a lesson, you horrible little brat!'

But then Pippi said:

'Actually, I haven't got time to play any longer. Although it's been lots of fun, I must admit.'

And with that she grabbed each policeman by the belt and carried them both through the front garden, out of the gate and onto the road. There she put them down on their feet, and it was a long time before either of them could move.

'Hang on a jiffy,' Pippi shouted, and she ran into the kitchen. She came out again with a couple of heart-shaped ginger biscuits, and said kindly:

'Would you like to try these? They're a bit burnt, hope you don't mind.'

Then she walked back to Tommy and Annika who were standing there in amazement, with eyes as big as saucers. And the policemen hurried back to town and told all the grown-ups that

Pippi probably wasn't suitable for a children's home. They didn't say they had been up on the roof. The grown-ups thought it was best to let Pippi go on living in Villa Villekulla. If she wanted to go to school she would have to make her own arrangements.

Pippi and Tommy and Annika had a really lovely afternoon. They continued their interrupted coffee party. Pippi managed to scoff fourteen ginger biscuits, and then she said:

'They weren't what I'd call proper policemen, oh no! Far too much talk about children's homes and multikipperation and Lisbon.'

Afterwards she lifted the horse from the veranda and they rode on him, all three together. Annika was afraid at first and didn't want to ride, but when she saw Pippi and Tommy enjoying themselves, she asked Pippi to hoist her up onto the horse's back too. The horse plodded round and round the garden, and Tommy sang: 'Watch out, here come the hurly-burly Swedes!'

When Tommy and Annika climbed into their beds that evening, Tommy said:

'Annika, don't you think it's brilliant that Pippi has moved in?'

'Of course I do,' said Annika.

'I can't even remember what we played before she came here, can you?'

'Oh, croquet and stuff,' said Annika. 'But it's always more fun with Pippi, I think. What with horses and everything!'

PIPPI GOES
TO SCHOOL

Naturally, Tommy and Annika went to school. Every morning at eight o'clock they wandered off hand in hand with their school books under their arm.

At that time Pippi was busy grooming her horse or getting Mr Nilsson dressed in his little suit. Or else she was doing her morning exercises, which involved standing bolt upright on the floor and turning forty-three somersaults one after the other. After that she would sit at her kitchen table and, in peace and quiet, drink a large cup of coffee and eat a cheese sandwich.

Tommy and Annika always looked longingly at Villa Villekulla as they trudged past on their way to school. They would much rather have been going to play with Pippi. If only Pippi had been going to school too. That would have made it more bearable.

'Think of all the fun we could have on our way home from school,' said Tommy.

'Yes, and on the way there, too,' said Annika.

The more they thought about Pippi not going to school, the worse they felt. Finally, they decided to try and talk her into going.

'We've got the best teacher ever, you have no idea,' said Tommy slyly, one afternoon, when he and Annika went round to Villa Villekulla after first doing their homework properly.

'If only you *knew* how much fun we have in school,' said Annika. 'I'd go potty if I wasn't allowed to go.'

Pippi was sitting on a stool, washing her feet in a basin. She didn't say anything. All she did was wiggle her big toe for a while, splashing water around her.

'You don't have to be there *that* long,' said Tommy. 'Only till two o'clock.'

'That's right, and you get Christmas holidays and Easter holidays and summer holidays,' said Annika.

Pippi bit her big toe, thinking hard but still not saying anything. Then without warning she tipped all the water out onto the kitchen floor so that Mr Nilsson, who was sitting nearby playing with a mirror, got his trousers soaked.

'It's unfair!' Pippi said crossly, ignoring how upset Mr Nilsson was about his wet trousers. 'It is absolutely unfair! I won't put up with it!'

'What?' asked Tommy.

'In four months it will be Christmas and you'll get a Christmas holiday. But what will I get?' Pippi sounded sad. 'No Christmas holiday, not even the teensy-weeniest little Christmas holiday,' she complained. 'Well, we'll soon change that. Tomorrow I start school.'

Tommy and Annika clapped their hands in delight.

'Hooray! We'll wait for you outside our front gate at eight tomorrow morning.'

'Oh, no,' said Pippi. 'I can't start that early. And anyway, I'll be riding to school.'

And that's exactly what she did. At ten o'clock on the dot the next day she lifted her horse down from the veranda, and a moment later everyone in the little town rushed to their windows to see the horse that had bolted—or so they thought. But it hadn't. It was only Pippi, in a hurry to get to school. Galloping wildly, she skidded into the school playground, jumped off the horse before it had stopped, tied him to a tree and flung open the school door with a crash that made Tommy and Annika and all their classmates jump at their desks.

'How-de-doo,' bellowed Pippi, waving her big hat. 'Have I come in time for multikipperation?'

Tommy and Annika had told their teacher that a new girl called Pippi Longstocking was going to turn up. The teacher had heard people in the town talking about Pippi, and because she was a very kind and friendly teacher she had decided to do all she could to make sure Pippi would be happy at school.

Pippi threw herself down at an empty desk without being told, but the teacher wasn't upset by her rude behaviour. She said, very kindly:

'Welcome to school, Pippi dear. I hope you will enjoy being here and that you will learn a lot.'

'Yes, and I hope I get a Christmas holiday as well,' said Pippi. 'That's why I've come. There must be some justice!'

'Perhaps first of all you would like to tell me your full name,' said the teacher. 'So I can write it in the register.'

'I'm called Pippilotta Victoriaria Tea-cosy Appleminta Ephraim's-daughter Longstocking, daughter of Captain Ephraim Longstocking, formerly the terror of the high seas and now a South Sea Island king. Pippi for short, because Dad thought Pippilotta was too long.'

'I see,' said the teacher. 'Then we shall also call you Pippi. Now, what about seeing how much you know?' she went on. 'You're a big girl and I'm sure you already know quite a lot. Let's start with arithmetic. Now, Pippi, can you tell me what you get if you add seven and five together?'

Pippi looked at her in astonishment. Then she said crossly:

'Well, if you don't know yourself I'm certainly not going to tell you.'

All the children stared at Pippi in horror. Then the teacher explained that she mustn't speak like that in school, and that she had to call the teacher 'Miss'.

'I'm ever so sorry,' said Pippi, apologetically. 'I didn't know. I won't do it again.'

'I hope not,' said the teacher. 'And I can tell you that seven plus five is twelve.'

'You see?' said Pippi. 'You knew it yourself, so

what did you ask me for? Oops, silly me, I forgot to say Miss. Sorry,' she said, and gave her ear a hard pinch.

The teacher decided to ignore that. She carried on:

'Well, Pippi, how much do you think eight plus four is?'

'Roughly sixty-seven,' guessed Pippi.

'No, it's not,' said the teacher. 'Eight plus four is twelve.'

'My good woman, I really have to say that now you're going too far,' said Pippi. 'You just said yourself that seven and five is twelve. There has to be some kind of order, even at school. Anyway, if you're so madly keen on that kind of nonsense, why don't you find a corner to sit in and do your sums, and leave us to play tag? Oh no, I forgot to call you Miss again!' she shrieked, horrified at herself. '*Can* you forgive me just this once? I'll *try* to behave better in future.'

The teacher said she would, but she didn't think there was any point trying to teach Pippi more arithmetic. She started asking the other children instead.

'Tommy, can you answer this?' she said. 'If Lisa

has seven apples and Axel has nine apples, how many apples do they have all together?'

'Yes, tell us, Tommy,' Pippi chimed in. 'And while you're at it you can tell me this: if Lisa gets a tummy ache and Axel gets even more of a tummy ache, whose fault is it and where did they scrump the apples from?'

The teacher tried to pretend she hadn't heard, and turned to Annika.

'Now, Annika, here's one for you. Gustav was with his friends on a school outing. He had one krona when he left and seven öre when he got home. How much had he spent?'

'Exactly,' said Pippi. 'I'd like to know why he wasted so much money, or if he bought lemonade, or if he washed behind his ears properly before he left home.'

The teacher decided to abandon arithmetic completely. She thought Pippi might be more interested in learning to read, which is why she showed them a beautiful little poster of an igloo. Beside the igloo was the letter 'i'.

'Now, Pippi, I'm going to show you something interesting,' she said gaily. 'This is an iiiiigloo, and the first letter is called "i".'

'Oh, I can't believe that,' said Pippi. 'It looks more like a straight line with fly poo at the top. And I would really like to know what an igloo has got to do with fly poo.'

The teacher showed them another poster with a picture of a snake and explained to Pippi that the first letter was 's'.

'Speaking of snakes,' Pippi said, 'I will never forget the time I fought a massive snake in India. You'd never believe how horrendous it was. Fourteen metres long and angry as a raging bull, and every day he ate up five Indian villagers with two little children for dessert, and once he came and wanted me for dessert, and he wound himself around me—squish—but, "I've seen a few things in my time," I said, and clobbered him on the head—bang—and then he hissed—hissshsshissss—and so I bashed him again—whack—and—errrgghhh—he died. So there you are, that's the letter "s" for you. Quite something!'

Pippi had to stop and catch her breath. And the teacher, who now thought Pippi was a troublesome and difficult child, suggested the class could do some drawing instead. Pippi was sure to sit still and draw nicely, thought the teacher. She handed

out paper and crayons to the children.

'You can draw whatever you like,' she said, and she sat down at her desk and began marking homework. After a while she looked up to see how they were getting on. All the children were sitting looking at Pippi, who was very happily drawing all over the floor.

'Oh, Pippi,' said the teacher, impatiently. 'Why aren't you drawing on the paper?'

'I filled that up ages ago. There's no room for my horse on that little piddling little piece of paper,' said Pippi. 'I'm in the middle of doing the front legs now, but when I get to the tail most likely I'll have to go out into the corridor.'

The teacher thought desperately for a few minutes.

'What if we sing a little song now, instead?' she suggested.

The children stood beside their desks, all except Pippi, who stayed where she was on the floor.

'You sing, by all means. I'll have a little rest here,' she said. 'Too much knowledge can send the sanest person completely bonkers.'

But now the teacher's patience had absolutely come to an end. She told all the children to go out into the playground because she wanted to have a talk with Pippi on her own.

When the teacher and Pippi were left alone Pippi stood up and walked to the teacher's desk at the front.

'Do you know something?' she said. 'I mean, do you know something, *Miss*? It was ever so much fun coming here to see what you get up to, but I don't think I'll bother coming to school again. Never mind about the Christmas holidays. There are far too many apples and igloos and snakes and things. It makes my head dizzy. I hope that doesn't upset you, Miss.'

But the teacher said she actually was upset, mostly because Pippi didn't want to try and behave properly, and no girl who carried on like Pippi would be able to go to school, however much she wanted to.

'Have I behaved badly?' asked Pippi, shocked. 'I really didn't know that,' she said, looking very sorrowful. No one could look as sorrowful as Pippi could when she was sad. She stood silently for a while and then said in a trembling voice:

'You see, Miss, when you have an angel for a mum and a South Sea Island king for a dad, and you've sailed around on the ocean all your life like me, then you don't really know how to behave in school among all those apples and igloos.'

Then the teacher said she realized that and she wasn't upset with Pippi any longer, and that perhaps Pippi could come back to school when she was a little older. Then Pippi said, beaming brightly:

'Oh Miss, I think you're so kind. And this is for you, Miss!'

From her pocket Pippi pulled out a lovely little gold watch which she lay on the teacher's desk. The teacher said she couldn't accept such a valuable gift from Pippi, but Pippi only said:

'You must! Otherwise I'll come back again tomorrow, and a fine spectacle that would be!'

Then Pippi dashed out to the playground and leapt onto her horse. All the children jostled around to pat the horse and watch her leave.

'Give me the schools in Argentina any day,' Pippi said, showing off. 'That's the place to be. There, the Easter holidays start three days after the Christmas holidays have finished, and three days after the Easter holidays it's time for the summer holidays. The summer holidays end on the first of November and then of course it's a struggle waiting for the Christmas holidays to start on the eleventh of November. But you can put up with it because there's no homework. Homework is strictly forbidden in Argentina. Now and then some Argentinian child sneaks into a wardrobe and sits there in secret, doing their homework, but pity them if their mum finds out. There's no arithmetic at all in the schools over there, and if any kid knows what seven and five is they have to stand in the naughty corner the whole day. If they're stupid enough to tell the teacher, that is. They only have reading on Fridays, and that's only if there are any books to read from. But there never are.'

'But what do they do in school, then?' a little boy asked.

'Eat sweets,' Pippi declared. 'A long pipe runs directly from a sweet factory close by and straight into the classroom, and sweets simply shoot out all day, so the children have more than enough to do eating sweets.'

'Yes, but, what do the teachers do?' asked a girl.

'Take the wrappers off the sweets for the children, you ninny,' said Pippi. 'You don't think they do that themselves, do you? I should say not! They don't even go to school themselves. They send their brother.'

Pippi waved her large hat.

'Cheerio kids!' she yelled gleefully. 'You won't be seeing me for a while. But always remember how many apples Axel had or you'll be sorry. Hahaha!'

With a resounding laugh, Pippi rode out of the playground so fast the gravel whirled around the horse's head and the school windows rattled.

PIPPI SITS ON
A GATE POST AND
CLIMBS A TREE

ippi, Tommy, and Annika were sitting outside Villa Villekulla. Pippi was on one gate post, Annika on the other, and Tommy was sitting on the gate. It was a beautiful warm day at the end of August. A pear tree next to the gate had branches growing so low down that the children could sit and pick the best yellowy-pink pears with no trouble at all. They munched and munched and spat the pear cores into the lane.

Villa Villekulla stood just where the small town finished and the countryside began, and where the street became a main road. The people of the town greatly enjoyed strolling out as far as Villekulla because it was in the prettiest part of town.

As the children were sitting there eating pears, a girl came walking along the street from the direction of town. When she caught sight of the children she stopped and said:

'Have you seen my dad go past?'

'Hmm,' said Pippi. 'What does he look like? Does he have blue eyes?'

'Yes,' said the girl.

'Medium height, not too tall, not too short?'

'Yes.'

'Black hat and black shoes?'

'Yes, exactly,' said the girl.

'No, we haven't seen him,' Pippi declared.

The girl looked disappointed and turned away without a word.

'Wait a minute,' Pippi shouted. 'Is he bald?'

'No, of course he isn't,' the girl said, crossly.

'Lucky for him,' said Pippi, and spat out a pear core. The girl hurried off, but Pippi shouted after her:

'Did he have unusually big ears that hung all the way down to his shoulders?'

'No,' said the girl, turning round in surprise. 'You don't mean you've seen a man walking past with ears that big?'

'I have never seen a man walking with ears,' Pippi said. 'Everyone I know walks with their feet.'

'Oh, how stupid you are. I mean have you really seen a man with such big ears?'

'Nope,' said Pippi. 'No one has such big ears. That would be absurd. What would it look like? You *can't* have ears that big. At least, not in this country,' she added, after pausing to think. 'In China it's a bit different. I saw one in Shanghai once, a Chinese man. His ears were so big he could use them like a cloak. When it rained he tucked himself under his ears and it was as warm and cosy as could be. Although not so much fun for his ears, of course. If the weather was particularly bad he would invite his friends and acquaintances to join him under his ears. There they sat, singing their mournful songs, waiting for the rain to go over. They were very fond of him because of his ears. Hai Shang was his name. You should have seen Hai Shang running to work every morning! He always came belting past at the last minute, because he loved sleeping late in the mornings, and you can't imagine how sweet it looked when he came running by with his ears like two huge yellow sails behind him.'

The girl had stopped walking and was listening to Pippi with her mouth wide open. And Tommy and Annika forgot all about eating pears. They were fully occupied with listening to Pippi, too.

'He had more children than he could count, and the youngest was called Petter.'

'What? A Chinese child can't be called Petter,' Tommy interrupted.

'That's exactly what his wife told him. "A Chinese child can't be called Petter," she said. But Hai Shang was so incredibly stubborn that he said the kid was to be called Petter or nothing. And he sat down in a corner, pulled his ears over his head and sulked. So then his poor wife had to agree, of course, and the kid was called Petter.'

'I see,' said Annika.

'He was the most contrary kid in the whole of Shanghai,' Pippi continued. 'So fussy with his food he drove his mum to tears. You know how they eat swallows' nests in China? Well, there was his mum with a whole bowlful of swallows' nests, ready to feed him. "Here, little Petter," she said. "Have one spoonful of bird's nest for Daddy!" But Petter simply clamped his mouth shut and shook his head. In the end Hai Shang was so angry that he said no more food was to be made for Petter until he had eaten one bird's nest for Daddy. And whatever Hai Shang said had to be done. The very same bird's nest was brought in and out of the kitchen from May to October. On the fourteenth of July his mother begged to give Petter a couple of meatballs, but Hai Shang said no.'

'Rubbish,' said the girl on the road.

'Yes, that's just what Hai Shang said,' continued Pippi. '"Rubbish!" he said. "Of course the child can eat the bird's nest, if only he would stop being so awkward." But Petter kept his mouth tight shut from May to October.'

'Then how could he survive?' Tommy asked, astonished.

'He couldn't survive,' said Pippi. 'He died. From absolute pig-headedness. On the eighteenth of October. Buried on the nineteenth. And on the twentieth a little swallow came flying in through the window and laid an egg in the nest on the table. So it came to good use anyway. No damage done,' Pippi said merrily. Then she stared at the girl, who was standing there, looking puzzled.

'You look very odd,' Pippi said. 'What's up? You don't think I'm lying, do you? What?! Come right out and tell me in that case,' threatened Pippi, rolling up her sleeves.

'No, no, not at all,' said the girl in alarm. 'I don't exactly mean you're lying, but . . .'

'You don't?' said Pippi. 'But that's exactly what I am doing. I'm lying so much my tongue's turning black, can't you tell? Do you honestly believe a kid can live without food from May to October? I mean, I know they can manage without food for three or four months, give or take, but from May to October? That's plain stupid. Surely you know that's a lie? You *mustn't* let people fool you into thinking any old thing.'

At that the girl walked off and didn't turn round again.

'People can be so gullible,' Pippi said to Tommy and Annika. 'From May to October, that's ridiculous.'

And she called after the girl:

'No, we haven't seen your dad! We haven't seen any baldies at all, not once all day. But yesterday seventeen walked past. Arm in arm!'

♥

Pippi's garden really was delightful. It wasn't well looked-after but there were lovely lawns that were never mown and old rose bushes that were full of white and yellow and pink roses. Not the most beautiful, it's true, but they had the most wonderful scent. Quite a few fruit trees grew there too, and—best of all—some very ancient oaks and elms that were perfect for climbing.

The trees in Tommy and Annika's garden weren't the climbing sort, and their mum was always afraid they might fall out of a tree and hurt themselves. That's why they hadn't done much climbing in their time. But Pippi said:

'What about climbing up that oak tree?'

Tommy immediately hopped down from the gate, overjoyed at the suggestion. Annika wasn't quite so sure, but when she saw the big bulges on the tree trunk that you could step on, she also thought it would be fun to try.

A couple of metres above the ground the tree divided into two branches, and in between it was just like a little room. It wasn't long before all three children were sitting there. Over their heads the oak spread out its canopy of leaves like a green roof.

'We could drink our coffee up here,' said Pippi. 'I'll pop in and make a cup or two.'

Tommy and Annika clapped their hands and cheered.

It wasn't long before Pippi had the coffee ready, and there were buns that she had made the day before. She stood below the oak tree and began flinging up the coffee cups. Tommy and Annika caught them. Sometimes the oak caught them, so two coffee cups broke, but Pippi ran indoors for some more. Then it was the turn of the buns, and for a long time the air was full of flying buns. At least they didn't break. Finally, Pippi climbed up with the coffee pot in one hand, cream in a bottle and sugar in a little box.

Tommy and Annika thought coffee had never tasted so good. They weren't usually allowed to drink coffee, only when they were visiting. And now they were visiting. Annika spilled some coffee on her knee. First it was warm and wet and then it was cold and wet, but that didn't matter, Annika said.

When they had finished Pippi sent the cups flying onto the grass below.

'I want to see how strong they make porcelain these days,' she said. One cup and all three plates landed safely, remarkably enough. And the coffee pot only lost its spout.

All at once Pippi thought she would climb
higher up the tree.

'Well I never!' she suddenly shouted. 'The tree
is hollow!'

There was a big hole that went right inside
the trunk. The leaves had kept it hidden from the
children.

'Oh, can I climb up as well and have a look?'
Tommy said. But he didn't get an answer. 'Pippi,
where are you?' he called anxiously.

Then they heard Pippi's voice, not from up above
but from deep down below, as if it was coming from
under the earth.

'I'm inside the tree. It's hollow right the way down to the ground. If I look out of a little crack I can see the coffee pot on the grass outside.'

'Oh, how are you going to get back up?' shouted Annika.

'I'm never coming up,' Pippi said. 'I'll stay here until I retire, and you'll have to throw food to me through the hole up there. Five or six times a day.'

Annika started crying.

'No more sorrow, no more tears,' said Pippi. 'Come down here instead, you two, and we can pretend we're languishing in a dungeon.'

'Not likely,' said Annika. And to be on the safe

side she climbed right the way down the tree.

'Annika, I can see you through the crack!' Pippi shouted. 'Don't tread on the coffee pot! It's a dear old coffee pot that's never done anyone any harm. And it's not its fault that it hasn't got a spout any longer.'

Annika walked up close to the tree and through a tiny gap she could see the very tip of Pippi's finger. It comforted her a lot to see it, but she was still worried.

'Pippi, can you really not get out?' she asked.

Pippi's finger disappeared and it took less than a minute for her head to pop out of the hole up in the tree.

'I might be able to if I try really hard,' she said, holding back the leafy branches.

'If it's that easy to get there,' said Tommy, who was still up in the tree, 'then I want to come down and languish a little bit too.'

'Hmm,' said Pippi. 'I think we ought to get a ladder.'

She heaved herself out of the hole and scrambled down to the ground. Then she ran to get a ladder, hauled it up into the tree and stuck it into the hole.

Tommy couldn't wait to climb down inside.

It was pretty difficult clambering up the tree to the hole because it was so high up, but Tommy was brave. And he wasn't afraid to step inside the dark tree trunk. Annika watched him disappear and she wondered if she would ever see him again. She tried looking through the gap.

'Annika,' she heard Tommy call. 'You'll never believe how wonderful it is. You've got to come in too. It isn't dangerous at all when you've got a ladder to climb on. Once you've done it you won't want to do anything else ever.'

'Are you sure?' Annika asked.

'Absolutely,' Tommy replied.

So, on wobbly legs, Annika climbed up the tree again, and Pippi helped her when she got to the difficult part. She shrank back when she saw how dark it was inside the tree trunk, but Pippi held her hand and encouraged her.

'Don't be afraid, Annika,' she heard Tommy say from below. 'I can see your legs now, and I'll catch you if you fall.'

But Annika didn't fall. She came down safe and sound to Tommy. And in a flash Pippi joined them.

'It's brilliant, isn't it?' said Tommy.

Annika had to agree that it was. It wasn't at all as dark as she had thought, because light was coming in through the gap. Annika went over to check that she could also see the coffee pot on the grass outside.

'We'll have this as our hiding place,' said Tommy. 'No one will know we're here. And if they walk up and down outside looking for us, we'll see them through the gap. And then we'll laugh.'

'We can have a little stick to poke out of the gap and tickle them,' said Pippi. 'They'll think it's haunted.'

This thought made the children so happy they hugged each other, all three together. Then they heard the gong from Tommy and Annika's house, telling them it was time for dinner.

'How stupid,' said Tommy. 'We've got to go home now. But we'll be back tomorrow, as soon as we're home from school.'

'Do that,' Pippi said.

So up the ladder they climbed again, first Pippi, then Annika, and last of all Tommy. And then they climbed down the tree, first Pippi, then Annika, and last of all Tommy.

PIPPI PLANS
AN OUTING

6 'We're not going to school today,' Tommy said to Pippi. 'They're scrubbing the floor so we've got the day off.'

'Ha!' yelled Pippi. 'Another injustice! I never get a day off for floor-scrubbing, although it's about time. Just look at the state of that kitchen floor! Still,' she added, 'when I think about it, I can scrub the floor anyway, day off or not. And that's exactly what I intend to do now. I'd like to see anyone try and stop me! Hop up on the kitchen table, you two, so you're out of the way.'

Tommy and Annika obediently climbed onto the table, and Mr Nilsson jumped up too and settled in Annika's lap.

Pippi heated a huge pan of water which she then tipped out all over the floor. After that she took off her long shoes and placed them neatly on the bread board. Then she tied two scrubbing brushes to her bare feet and skated around the floor, spraying water everywhere.

'I really should have been a skating princess,' she said, and lifted one leg straight into the air so that the scrubbing brush on her left foot broke off a piece of the ceiling lamp.

'I am graceful and charming, if nothing else,' she went on, leaping swiftly over a chair that was in her way.

'There we are, all clean now,' she said at last, and took off the brushes.

'Aren't you going to mop up the water?' Annika asked.

'No, it can dry in the sun,' Pippi said. 'I don't think it will get a cold as long as it keeps moving.'

Tommy and Annika clambered down from the table and stepped as carefully as they could over the floor, trying not to get wet.

Outside the sun was shining from a clear blue sky. It was one of those glorious September days when you feel you want to go walking in the forest. Pippi had an idea.

66

'What if we take Mr Nilsson with us and go on an outing?'

'Yes!' shouted Tommy and Annika.

'Then run home and ask your mum,' said Pippi. 'While I make a picnic for us.'

Tommy and Annika thought that was a good idea. They shot off home and it wasn't long before they were back again. Pippi was already standing by the gate with Mr Nilsson on her shoulder, a walking pole in one hand and a large basket in the other.

The children walked beside the main road for a while but then turned off into a meadow where a nice little path wound its way between birch trees and hazelnut bushes. Eventually they came to a gate and behind the gate was a meadow that was even more beautiful than the first one. However, a cow was standing right beside the gate, blocking their way, and she didn't look as if she was planning to move. Annika shouted at her and Tommy bravely walked up and tried to shoo her away, but she didn't budge an inch. All she did was stare at the children with her big cow eyes. To bring an end to it all Pippi put down the picnic basket, walked up, and lifted the cow out of the way. Rather embarrassed, the cow shuffled off between the hazelnut bushes.

'To think that cows can be so pig-headed,' said Pippi, leaping over the gate with both feet at once. 'And what is the result? That pigs become cow-headed, of course! It's quite scary to think of it.'

'Such a beautiful, beautiful meadow,' shouted Annika in delight, and stepped onto every rock she saw. Tommy had brought along the knife Pippi had given him, and he cut walking poles for himself and Annika. He cut his thumb a little, too, but that didn't matter.

'We might as well pick some mushrooms while we're here,' said Pippi, and broke off a beautiful red death cap toadstool. 'I wonder if you can eat this?' she continued. 'You can't drink it, at least, I know that much, so there's no other choice but to eat it. Maybe you can!'

She bit off a huge chunk of the toadstool and swallowed it.

'I could!' she said happily. 'Well, well. We'll most definitely take this home and cook it another day,' she said, and hurled the toadstool high over the treetops.

'What's in the basket, Pippi?' asked Annika. 'Is

it something delicious?'

'I wouldn't tell you for a thousand kronor,' Pippi said. 'First we'll find a good place to spread it out.'

The children eagerly began searching for such a place. Annika found a large, flat rock which she thought was suitable, but it was full of red ants crawling about.

'I'm not sitting with them, I don't know them,' said Pippi.

'Yes, and they bite as well,' said Tommy.

'Do they?' said Pippi. 'Well, bite back!'

Then Tommy caught sight of a small glade between a couple of hazelnut bushes, and he thought they should sit there.

'Oh no, it's not sunny enough, my freckles wouldn't like it,' said Pippi. 'And I think freckles are most attractive.'

A short way off was a little rocky hill which was easy to climb, and on the hill was a sunny, flat place, just like a balcony. That's where they sat down.

'Now close your eyes while I lay it all out,' said Pippi. Tommy and Annika screwed up their eyes as tightly as they could. They heard Pippi open the basket, and they heard the rustle of paper.

'One, two, nineteen, you can look now,' said Pippi at last.

So they looked, and they shrieked in delight when they saw all the tasty things Pippi had laid out on the bare rock. There were lovely little sandwiches made with meatballs and ham, a whole heap of pancakes dusted with sugar, some small brown sausages, and three pineapple puddings. Because, you see, the chef on Pippi's father's boat had shown her how to cook.

'Oh, it's so nice having a floor-scrubbing day,' said Tommy, with his mouth full of pancake. 'We should have one every day.'

'No, I don't think so,' said Pippi. 'I'm not that mad about scrubbing floors. It's fun, I'll give you that, but not every day. That would be boring.'

Eventually the children were so full they could hardly move, so they sat still and enjoyed the sunshine.

'I wonder if it's hard to fly,' said Pippi, looking over the edge, lost in thought. The rock face dropped steeply below them and it was a long way to the ground.

'You could probably learn to fly down,' she

went on. 'But flying up would be worse. Better to start with the easiest way. I think I'll try.'

'No, Pippi!' yelled Tommy and Annika together. 'Oh, please, Pippi, don't do it!'

But Pippi was already standing on the edge.

'Fly, you flappy fly, fly, and the flappy fly flew,' she said, and just as she said 'flew' she raised her arms and stepped out into thin air. After half a second there was a thud. It was Pippi, hitting the ground. Tommy and Annika lay on their stomachs, peering down at her in terror. Pippi stood up and brushed off her knees.

'I forgot to flap,' she said happily. 'And I think I had too many pancakes in my tummy.'

Just at that moment the children realized that Mr Nilsson was missing. He had clearly set off on a little outing of his own. They remembered seeing him cheerfully chewing the picnic basket to pieces, but during Pippi's flying practice they had completely forgotten about him. And now he was gone.

Pippi was so angry that she threw one of her shoes into a large, deep puddle.

'You should never take monkeys with you when you go anywhere,' she said. 'He really should have stayed at home, de-fleaing the horse. That would have served him right,' she said, stepping into the puddle to collect her shoe. The water came up to her middle.

'I suppose I might as well wash my hair while I'm at it,' Pippi said, and dipped her head under the water for so long that bubbles started coming to the surface.

'There, no need to go to the hairdresser's for a while,' she said contentedly, when she finally reappeared. She stepped out of the puddle and put her shoe back on. Then off they went to look for Mr Nilsson.

'Listen to the squelching I make when I walk,' she laughed. 'My dress is going "slap, slap", and my shoes are going "squelch, squelch". It's really funny. I think you should try it too,' she said to Annika, who was walking along so prettily with her shiny blonde curls, pink dress and small, white leather shoes.

'Another time,' said sensible Annika.

They walked on.

'We have good reason to be angry with Mr Nilsson,' said Pippi. 'He's always doing this. He ran away from me once in Surabaya and took a job as a housekeeper to an old widow lady. That last bit was a lie, of course,' she added, after a pause.

Tommy suggested they should each go in a different direction to look. Annika didn't want to at first, but Tommy said:

'You aren't scared, are you?'

Naturally, Annika wasn't prepared to tolerate such an insult, so off all three went on their separate paths.

Tommy's path took him across a field. He didn't find Mr Nilsson, but he found something else. A bull! Or, to be more exact, the bull found him, and the bull didn't like Tommy because he was an angry bull that wasn't too keen on children. He came charging up with his head lowered, bellowing unpleasantly, and Tommy let out a yell of terror that could be heard throughout the forest. Pippi and Annika heard it too and came running up to see why Tommy had yelled. By that time the bull had already caught Tommy on its horns and tossed him high in the air.

'Such a foolish bull,' Pippi said to Annika, who was sobbing inconsolably. 'That's really no way to behave. He'll get Tommy's white sailor suit all dirty. I must go and talk some sense into the pesky animal.'

And so she did. She ran up to the bull and pulled its tail.

'Excuse me for breaking in,' she said, and because she pulled hard the bull turned round and saw another child he thought he'd toss on his horns.

'As I said, excuse me for breaking in,' Pippi said again. 'And excuse me for breaking off,' she added, and she broke off one of the bull's horns. 'It isn't fashionable to have *two* horns this year,' she said. 'This year the better kind of bull has only *one* horn. If they have any at all,' she said, and broke off the other one as well.

Because a bull has no feeling in its horns the animal didn't know its horns had gone. It butted and butted its head, and if it had been anyone other than Pippi that child would have been pulp by this time.

'Hahaha, stop tickling me,' shouted Pippi. 'You have no idea how ticklish I am. Haha, stop it, stop it, I'll kill myself laughing!'

But the bull didn't stop, and finally Pippi leapt up onto its back to get a moment's peace. She didn't get that much peace, of course, because the bull didn't like having Pippi on his back. He bucked and threw himself around wildly to try and get her off, but she simply held on tighter with her legs and stayed where she was. The bull charged backwards and forwards across the field, bellowing so much that steam came pouring out of his nostrils. Pippi laughed and shrieked and waved to Tommy and Annika, who were standing some distance away, trembling like aspen leaves. The bull whirled round and round and tried to throw Pippi off.

'Here I am, dancing with my little friend,' sang Pippi, glued to its back. Eventually the bull grew so tired that he lay down on the ground, wishing there were no such things as little children on this earth. He had never thought children were especially necessary, anyway.

'Are you thinking of having an afternoon nap now?' Pippi asked politely. 'In which case, I won't disturb you.'

She stepped off his back and walked over to Tommy and Annika. Tommy had been crying a little. He had a cut on one arm, but Annika had wound her handkerchief around it so it didn't hurt any longer.

'Oh, Pippi!' Annika said frantically, when Pippi came back.

'Shhh,' whispered Pippi. 'Don't wake the bull! He's sleeping and if we wake him up that will only make him grumpy.'

'Mr Nilsson, Mr Nilsson, where are you?' she yelled loudly the very next second, not caring about the bull's afternoon nap. 'We've got to go home.'

And sure enough, there sat Mr Nilsson, curled up in a pine tree. He was sucking the end of his tail and looking miserable. It wasn't much fun for such a little monkey to be left alone in the forest. He scampered down from the tree and up onto Pippi's shoulder, and waved his straw hat the way he always did when he was really happy.

'So, you decided not to become a housekeeper this time,' said Pippi, stroking his back. 'Bother, that truly was a lie,' she added. 'But, if it was truly, it couldn't be a lie,' she said, thinking it over. 'You see, when it comes down to it, he really was a housekeeper in Surabaya after all! And now I know who's going to make the meatballs from now on.'

They wandered homewards, with Pippi's dress still slapping and her shoes still squelching. Tommy and Annika thought it had been a wonderful day, despite the bull, and they sang a song they had learned at school. It was a summer song really, and it would soon be autumn, but they thought it would do very well anyway.

We're walking in the sunshine
and singing as we go,
You never hear us moaning,
We're singing as we go, hello, hello!
Hey everyone, join in the song
Don't sit at home, lazy and alone.
We never stop,
Walking to the top
Of the highest hill, up and up and up.
We're walking in the sunshine
and singing as we go, hello, hello!

Pippi joined in, but she didn't sing quite the same words. Her song went like this:

I'm walking in the sunshine
And singing as I go.
I do just what I want to
But I'm squelching as I go, squelch
Squosh, squelch squosh!
But oh, my shoes, golly and gosh
They're going squelch and splosh and
squelch and splosh.
Cos my shoes are wet
And the bull's a pest,
And I love rice pudding the best.
I'm walking in the sunshine
And squelching as I go, squish squosh,
squish squosh!

PIPPI GOES
TO THE CIRCUS

A circus had come to the little town and all the children ran to their mums and dads and pleaded to be allowed to go. Tommy and Annika did the same, and their kind dad soon took out a few shiny silver kronor coins and handed them to the children.

With the money tightly clutched in their hands they raced off to Pippi's house. She was on the veranda with the horse. She was braiding his tail into lots of tiny plaits, which she tied with red bows.

'It's his birthday today, I think,' she said. 'So he has to look smart.'

'Pippi,' Tommy panted, because they had run fast, 'Pippi, do you want to go along to the circus?'

'I can go along with anything,' said Pippi. 'But whether I can go along to Sir Cuss, I don't know, because I don't know who Sir Cuss is. Is he nice?'

'Don't be silly,' said Tommy. 'It's not a person! It's something you watch and it's lots of fun! Horses, clowns, and pretty ladies walking on a tightrope.'

'But it costs money,' said Annika, and she opened her small hand to see if the large, shiny two-kronor coin and the two fifty-öre coins were still there.

'I'm as rich as a king,' said Pippi. 'So I expect I could afford to buy a Sir Cuss. Though it will be tricky if I'm going to have more horses. The clowns and the tightrope walkers can squeeze into the laundry shed, but the horses will be a problem.'

'Chump,' said Tommy. 'A circus isn't something you buy. It costs money to go there and look, didn't you know?'

'Scupper me!' shouted Pippi, and snapped her eyes shut. 'Does it cost money to look? And here's me, going around looking every day! Who knows how much money I have spent looking at things by now?'

Gradually she opened one eye, very cautiously, and rolled it round and round. 'Well, whatever it costs,' she said. 'I've just got to have a look!'

Eventually Tommy and Annika managed to explain to Pippi what a circus was, and then Pippi went to her travelling bag and took out some gold coins. After that she put on her hat that was as big as a cartwheel and off they trooped to the circus.

Hordes of people were milling around the circus tent and there was a long queue at the ticket office. But at last it was Pippi's turn. She shoved her head in the ticket hatch, stared at the dear old lady sitting behind it, and said:

'How much does it cost to look at you, then?'

But the old lady was from another country and she didn't understand what Pippi meant. So she answered:

'Leetel girl, it cost five kwoner best seat, three kwoner second-best seat, one kwona in the shtanding.'

'I see,' said Pippi. 'Then you've got to promise to walk the tightrope too.'

Tommy took over and told Pippi to get a second-best seat. Pippi held out a gold coin and the old lady looked at it suspiciously. She bit it, too, to see if it was genuine. Finally she was convinced that it really was gold, and Pippi got her ticket. She got a whole lot of silver coins back in change as well.

'What am I going to do with all these nasty little white things?' Pippi said, irritably. 'Keep them, why don't you? Then I can look at you twice instead. In the shtanding.'

Since Pippi absolutely refused to have any money back, the lady exchanged her ticket for one in the front row, and she also gave Tommy and Annika front row seats without charging them anything at all. That was how Pippi, Tommy and Annika came to sit on some very fine red seats right beside the circus arena. Tommy and Annika turned round several times to wave at their school friends who were sitting much further back.

'This is a weird kind of tent,' said Pippi, looking around in astonishment. 'And they've spilled sawdust on the floor, I see. Not that I'm so particular, but it looks untidy, I think.'

Tommy explained to Pippi that all circuses had sawdust on the floor for the horses to gallop around on.

Up on a balcony sat the circus orchestra who suddenly burst into a loud, exhilarating march. Pippi clapped madly and jumped up and down in her chair with excitement.

'Does it cost to hear as well or do you get that free?' she asked.

Just then the curtain to the performers' entrance was pulled aside and the ringmaster in a black tailcoat and carrying a whip came running in, along with ten white horses with red plumes on their heads.

The ringmaster cracked the whip and the horses galloped round the ring. Then the ringmaster cracked the whip again and all the horses stood with their front legs on the barrier surrounding the ring. One of the horses had stopped right in front of the children's seats. Annika didn't like having a horse so close to her and she shrank back in her chair as far as she could. But Pippi leaned forwards, lifted the horse's front leg and said:

'Well, hello there! And hello from *my* horse. It's his birthday today but he's got bows in his tail instead of on his head.'

Luckily Pippi dropped the horse's foot before the ringmaster cracked his whip again, because when he did that all the horses jumped down from the barrier and began galloping again.

When the act was finished the ringmaster bowed

politely and the horses ran out. The next instant the curtain opened again to reveal a brilliantly white horse, and on its back stood a beautiful lady dressed in a green silk outfit. Her name was Miss Carmencita, so the programme said.

The horse trotted around in the sawdust and Miss Carmencita stood serenely on its back, smiling. But then something happened. Just as the horse passed Pippi's seat, something came swooshing through the air, and it was none other than Pippi herself. And there she stood, on the horse's back, behind Miss Carmencita. At first Miss Carmencita was so astonished she almost fell off the horse. Then she got angry. She began hitting out behind her to make Pippi jump off. But she didn't succeed.

'Calm down a litre or two! You can't have all the fun. Some people have paid, you know!'

That made Miss Carmencita want to jump off, but that didn't work either because Pippi was clinging to her waist. The people in the audience couldn't help laughing. It looked so ridiculous, they thought, with the beautiful Miss Carmencita grabbed tight by a little red-haired kid who was standing on the horse's back in her big shoes,

looking as if she had never done anything else but perform in a circus all her life.

But the ringmaster didn't laugh. He made a sign to his security guards in their red suits to run up and stop the horse.

'Oh, is the act over already?' said Pippi, disappointed. 'Just when we were having such fun!'

'You very bad, bad girl,' hissed the ringmaster between gritted teeth. 'Go avay.'

Pippi looked at him in dismay.

'What's wrong?' she said. 'Why are you angry with me? I thought the idea was to have fun.'

She slid off the horse and went and sat in her seat. But two huge security guards came to throw her out. They took hold of her and tried to lift her up.

They couldn't. Pippi sat perfectly still and wouldn't budge, even though they heaved as hard as they could. So they shrugged their shoulders and walked off.

Meanwhile the next act had started. It was Miss Elvira, the tightrope walker. She was wearing a pink net tutu and had a pink parasol in her hand. With small, dainty steps she ran out onto the tightrope. She kicked her legs and performed all kinds of tricks. It looked very pretty. She even showed that she could walk backwards on the narrow tightrope. But when she returned to the little platform at one end and turned around, there was Pippi.

'Surprise, surprise,' said Pippi, delighted to see Miss Elvira's astonished expression.

Miss Elvira said nothing. All she did was jump down from the tightrope and throw her arms around the ringmaster, who was her father. And the ringmaster once again sent his security guards to throw Pippi out. This time he sent five.

But then everyone watching the circus cried out:

'Leave her alone! We want to see the red-haired lass!'

And they stamped their feet and clapped their hands.

Pippi ran out onto the tightrope. Miss Elvira's tricks were nothing compared to Pippi's. When she came to the middle she stuck one leg up in the air and her big shoe was like a roof over her head. She bent her foot a little so she could scratch herself behind the ear with it.

The ringmaster was not at all pleased to have Pippi performing in his circus. He wanted to get rid of her. Which is why he crept up and loosened the mechanism that kept the rope tight, certain that Pippi would fall down.

But Pippi didn't. She simply used the rope as a swing. To and fro she went, swinging faster and faster and then—all of a sudden—she leapt into the air and landed right on top of the ringmaster. He was so afraid he started running.

'This is a jolly old horse,' said Pippi. 'But why hasn't it got any bows in its hair?'

By now Pippi thought it was time to go back to Tommy and Annika. She slid off the ringmaster's back and went and sat down. Now it was time for the next act. It was delayed for a while because the ringmaster had to go out and drink a glass of water and comb his hair.

But he came back into the ring, bowed to the audience and said:

'Ladees and gentlemen! In a few moments you vill be able to vatch the greatesht miracle off all time, the shtrongest man in the world. Shtrong Adolf, who no one has ever beatens. May I present, ladees and gentlemen, Shtrong Adolf!'

And into the ring strode an enormous man. He was wearing flesh-coloured tights and had a leopard skin round his waist. He bowed to the audience and looked very pleased with himself.

'Jusht look at his mushles,' said the ringmaster, and felt Strong Adolf's arm where the muscles swelled like bowling balls under his skin.

'And now, ladees and gentelmen, I make my finesht offer! Who among you dares to take on Shtrong Adolf in the vrestling match? Who dares to try and beat the vorld's shtrongest man? One huntret kwoner to him who beat Shtrong Adolf. Huntret kwoner, think of that, ladees and gentelmen! Please, shtep up! Who will shtep up?'

No one stepped up.

'What did he say?' asked Pippi. 'And why is he speaking Greek?'

'He said that anyone who can beat that massive man will get a hundred kronor,' said Tommy.

'I can do it,' said Pippi. 'But I think it's a pity to fight him. He looks so kind.'

'But you can't do that, surely?' said Annika. 'He's the world's strongest man!'

'*Man*, yes,' said Pippi. 'But I am the world's strongest girl, remember that!'

While he was waiting, Strong Adolf was lifting huge balls of iron and bending iron bars to show how strong he was.

'Well, everyone,' bellowed the ringmaster. 'Is there really nobody who vant to earn huntret kwonor? Shall I really haf to keep them for myshelf?' he asked, waving the hundred kronor note about.

'Not if *I* can help it,' said Pippi, and climbed over the barrier and into the ring.

The ringmaster flew into a frenzy when he spotted her.

'Go! Dishappear! You I do not vant to see,' he hissed.

'Why do you always have to be so unfriendly?' Pippi scolded him. 'All I want to do is fight Strong Adolf.'

'This is not the place for your yokings,' said the ringmaster. 'Go avay, before Shtrong Adolf hear your impertinensh.'

But she walked straight past the ringmaster and up to Strong Adolf. She took hold of his big hand and shook it warmly.

'Now we're going to have a little tussle, you and me,' she said.

Strong Adolf stared at her and wondered what was going on.

'I'll start in one minute,' said Pippi.

And so she did. She held Strong Adolf in a firm grip and before he knew how it happened she had flung him down on the mat. Strong Adolf shot up, all red in the face.

'Come on, Pippi!' yelled Tommy and Annika. All the people at the circus heard that, and they shouted 'Come on, Pippi!' as well. The ringmaster sat on the barrier and wrung his hands. He was furious. But Strong Adolf was even more furious. Never in his entire life had he experienced anything so outrageous. Now that little red-haired kid would see what kind of man Strong Adolf was! He rushed at her and grabbed her round the waist. But Pippi stood as solid as a rock.

'You can do better than that,' she said, to encourage him. But then she slipped out of his grasp and in a flash Strong Adolf was lying on the mat again. Pippi stood beside him, waiting. She didn't have to wait long. With a yell he got up and stormed towards her.

'Tum-tee-tum-tee-tum,' said Pippi.

Everyone in the audience stamped their feet

and threw their hats into the air and shouted: 'Come on, Pippi!'

When Strong Adolf came rushing towards her for the third time, Pippi picked him up and carried him high in the air all around the ring. Then she lay him down on the mat again and held him there.

'Now, young fellow, I think we've had about enough,' she said. 'It won't get much more entertaining than this.'

'Pippi wins, Pippi wins!' shouted all the people at the circus. Strong Adolf loped off as fast as he could. And the ringmaster was obliged to hand Pippi the hundred kronor note, although he looked as if he would rather eat her up.

'Here you are, leetel miss,' he said. 'One huntret kwonor!'

'That?' sneered Pippi. 'What do I want with that bit of paper? You can have it to wrap herrings in, if you want.'

And she returned to her seat.

'It's a very long Sir Cuss, isn't it?' she said to Tommy and Annika. 'A little nap wouldn't hurt. But wake me up if I can help with anything.'

And she leaned back in her seat and fell fast

asleep. There she lay, snoring, while the clowns and the sword swallowers and the snake charmers performed their tricks for Tommy and Annika and everyone in the audience.

'But I still think Pippi was best,' whispered Tommy to Annika.

PIPPI HAS
A VISIT
FROM THIEVES

After Pippi's performance at the circus there wasn't a single person in the little town who didn't know how tremendously strong she was. She was even in the newspaper. But naturally, people who lived anywhere else didn't know who Pippi was.

One dark autumn evening two vagabonds came wandering along the road past Villa Villekulla. The vagabonds were two nasty thieves who were roaming all around the country to see if they could find anything to pinch. They saw the lights on in Villa Villekulla's windows and decided to go in and ask for a sandwich.

Now, that very evening Pippi had tipped out all her gold coins onto the kitchen floor and was sitting there counting them. She couldn't count all that well, it's true, but even so she did it from time to time. Just to keep things in order.

'. . . seventy-five, seventy-six, seventy-seven, seventy-eight, seventy-nine, seventy-ten, seventy-eleven, seventy-twelve, seventy-thirteen, seventy-seventeen . . . urgh, my mouth's all seventyish! Scupper me, there must be *other* numblers to choose from . . . of course, I remember now, a hundred and four, one thousand. That's an awful lot of money indeed,' said Pippi.

Just then there was a loud banging on the door.

'Come in or stay where you are, it's entirely up to you,' called Pippi. 'I never force anyone!'

The door opened and the two vagabonds came in. Imagine their faces when they saw a little red-haired girl sitting there all alone on the floor, counting money!

'Are you at home all on your own?' they asked, slyly.

'Not at all,' said Pippi. 'Mr Nilsson is at home as well.'

Of course, the thieves couldn't know that Mr Nilsson was a little monkey who at that moment was fast asleep under a doll's blanket in his green-painted bed. They thought the man of the house was called Nilsson and they winked at each other knowingly.

'We can come back a little later,' the wink meant, but to Pippi all they said was:

'Oh, we only came in to ask about the time.'

They were so excited they forgot all about asking for sandwiches.

'Big strong men who don't know about the time?' said Pippi. 'What kind of upbringing have you had, exactly? The time is on a round thingummy that says tick tock and goes and goes and never gets anywhere. If you've got any other riddles, let's hear them,' she said, encouragingly.

The thieves thought Pippi was too young to know how to tell the time, so they turned without a word and went out again.

'I don't expect you to say thank you,' shouted Pippi. 'But you could at least say tick-tock and toodle-oo! But, all the same, safe journey!'

Once they were outside the thieves rubbed their hands with joy.

'Did you see all that money? Jeepers creepers!' said one of them.

'Yes, what a stroke of luck,' said the other. 'All

we've got to do now is wait for the little girl and that Nilsson fellow to go to sleep. Then we creep in and get our mitts on the lot of it.'

They sat down under an oak tree in the garden to wait. It was drizzling with rain and they were very hungry so it really wasn't very pleasant, but the thought of all that money kept their spirits up.

The lights in all the houses went out one by one, all except for Villa Villekulla. That's because

Pippi was teaching herself to dance the polka and didn't want to go to bed until she was sure she knew how to do it. But at last even the lights in Villa Villekulla went out.

The vagabonds waited a good while to make sure that Mr Nilsson had fallen asleep. But finally they tiptoed to the kitchen door and got ready to open it with their break-in tools. One of them—his name was Bloom, by the way—

happened by pure chance to feel the handle. The door wasn't locked.

'People must be mad,' he whispered to his mate. 'The door's open!'

'So much the better for us,' answered his companion, a dark-haired man who went by the name of Thunder-Karlsson to those who knew him.

Thunder-Karlsson switched on his torch and they both slunk into the kitchen. There was no one there. The next room was Pippi's bedroom, and Mr Nilsson's little doll's bed was there too. Thunder-Karlsson opened the door and cautiously peered in. It was calm and quiet and he ran the beam of his torch round the room. When the beam of light reached Pippi's bed, both vagabonds saw to their amazement nothing other than a pair of feet resting on the pillow. As usual, Pippi had her head under the covers at the foot end of the bed.

'It must be that little girl,' Thunder-Karlsson whispered to Bloom. 'And now she's fast asleep. But where is Nilsson, do you think?'

'*Mr* Nilsson, if you don't mind,' came Pippi's calm voice from under the covers. 'Mr Nilsson is sleeping in the little green doll's bed.'

The men were so startled they turned to rush out immediately. But then they realized what Pippi had said, that Mr Nilsson was lying in the doll's bed. In the light of the torch they caught sight of the doll's bed with the tiny monkey. Thunder-Karlsson couldn't help laughing.

'Bloom,' he said. 'Mr Nilsson is a monkey, hahaha!'

'Well, what did you think he was?' came Pippi's voice again from under the covers. 'A lawnmower?'

'Aren't your mum and dad at home?' asked Bloom.

'Nope,' said Pippi. 'They're gone! Completely gone!'

Thunder-Karlsson and Bloom were so delighted they chuckled to themselves.

'Now listen here, little girl,' said Thunder-Karlsson. 'Come out so we can have a chat.'

'No, I'm asleep,' said Pippi. 'Is it about riddles again? Because if so, you can answer this one first: what kind of clock keeps going and going and never reaches the door?'

But Bloom, without waiting any longer, pulled the covers off Pippi.

'Can you dance the polka?' she asked, looking him very seriously in the eye. 'I can!'

'You ask too many questions,' Thunder-Karlsson said. 'Perhaps we can also ask a few. For example, where is the money that was spread all over the floor just now?'

'In my travelling bag on top of the cupboard,' Pippi answered, truthfully.

Thunder-Karlsson and Bloom grinned.

'I hope you don't mind if we take it, my dear,' said Thunder-Karlsson.

'Since you ask,' said Pippi. 'Of course not!'

At that Bloom walked over and took down the travelling bag.

'And I hope you don't mind if I take it back again, my dear,' said Pippi, and she climbed out of bed and went up to Bloom.

Bloom didn't really know how it happened but, lickety-spit, there was the bag in Pippi's hand.

'Stop larking about,' said Thunder-Karlsson angrily. 'Hand over the bag!'

He took hold of Pippi's arm hard and tried to grab the loot he so desperately wanted.

'Larking about? I'll give you larking about,' said Pippi, and she lifted up Thunder-Karlsson and sat him on top of the cupboard. The next second Bloom was sitting beside him. That made both the vagabonds afraid. They began to realize that Pippi was no ordinary girl. But the bag of money was so tempting it made them forget their fear.

'Now, Bloom!' shouted Thunder-Karlsson, and they jumped down from the cupboard and threw themselves over Pippi, who was holding the bag in her hand. But Pippi prodded them with her index finger and they ended up in opposite corners of the room. Before they had time to stand up, Pippi had found a rope and quick as lightning tied it round the thieves' arms and legs. They soon changed their tune.

'Dear, sweet little girl,' begged Thunder-Karlsson. 'Forgive us, we were only joking! Don't hurt us, we're only two poor wanderers who came in looking for some food.'

Bloom even began shedding a few tears.

Pippi put the bag back on top of the cupboard. Then she turned to face her two prisoners.

'Can either of you dance the polka?'

'We-e-ell,' said Thunder-Karlsson. 'We both can. Sort of.'

'Oh, what fun!' Pippi clapped her hands. '*Please* let's have a quick dance. I've just learnt how to do it, you see.'

'Well, I suppose we could,' said Thunder-Karlsson, somewhat baffled.

Then Pippi found a large pair of scissors and cut the rope that was tied around her guests.

'Oh, we haven't got any music,' said Pippi, looking disappointed. Then she had an idea.

'You can play on a comb and paper,' she said to Bloom. 'While I dance with him.' She pointed at Thunder-Karlsson.

Oh yes, Bloom knew how to play on a comb all right. And it echoed through the whole house when he did. Mr Nilsson sat up in his bed, woken-up and sleepy, just in time to see Pippi whirl round and round with Thunder-Karlsson. She was deadly serious and she danced very fast, as if her life depended on it.

Eventually Bloom didn't want to play the comb any more because he said it tickled his mouth something terrible. And Thunder-Karlsson had been tramping along the roads all day and his legs were starting to get tired.

'Please, just a *little* longer,' Pippi begged, and

carried on dancing. And Bloom and Thunder-Karlsson had no choice but to continue.

When it was three o'clock in the morning, Pippi said:

'Oh, I could carry on until Thursday! But perhaps you're tired and hungry?'

That is exactly what they were, although they hardly dared say so. But from the larder Pippi brought out bread and cheese, butter and ham and sliced beef to eat, and milk to drink, and they all sat around the table. Bloom and Thunder-Karlsson and Pippi ate and ate until they almost burst. Pippi poured some milk into her ear.

'It's good for ear infections,' she said.

'Ah, poor thing, have you got an ear infection?' asked Bloom.

'No,' said Pippi. 'But I might.'

Finally, both the vagabonds stood up, thanked Pippi heartily for the food and asked if they could leave.

'It was *so* nice of you to come! Do you *have* to go so soon?' Pippi said, disappointed.

'I have never seen anyone who can dance the polka as well as you, my little pumpkin,' she said to Thunder-Karlsson.

'Practise hard,' she said to Bloom. 'And you'll find playing the comb won't tickle quite so much.'

As they were standing in the doorway, Pippi rushed up to them and gave them a gold coin each.

'You honestly deserve it,' she said.

PIPPI GOES TO A COFFEE PARTY

Tommy and Annika's mother had invited a few ladies for a coffee party, and because she had baked more than enough cakes and biscuits she thought Tommy and Annika could invite Pippi as well. She would have less trouble with her own children that way, she thought.

Tommy and Annika were over the moon when they heard this, and they immediately ran to Pippi's house to invite her. Pippi was working in her garden, watering the few straggly flowers with a rusty old watering can. Since the rain was bucketing down that day, Tommy told Pippi he thought it was entirely unnecessary.

'That's what you think,' said Pippi, annoyed.

'I've been lying awake all night, looking forward to getting up and doing the watering, and a little rain isn't going to stop me, I can tell you!'

Then Annika told her the good news about the coffee party.

'Coffee party . . . me?' yelped Pippi, and she became so anxious that she started watering Tommy instead of the rose bush she was supposed to be watering. 'Oh, what will it be like? Oh, I'm so nervous! What if I can't behave myself?'

'Of course you can,' said Annika.

'Don't be so sure,' said Pippi. 'I do try, believe you me, but I have noticed from time to time that people think I can't behave, even though I've been trying ever so hard. At sea we weren't too particular about such things. But I promise I will make a real effort so you won't have to be ashamed of me.'

'Super,' said Tommy, and he and Annika shot back home again through the rain.

'This afternoon, three o'clock. Don't forget!' yelled Annika, as she peeped out from under the umbrella.

At three o'clock that afternoon a very elegant lady walked up the steps to the Settergren family's front door. It was Pippi Longstocking. For once her red hair was not in plaits and it fell like a lion's mane around her head. She had painted her mouth bright red with a crayon, and coloured her eyebrows black, which made her look almost dangerous. With the same red crayon she had painted her nails, and on her shoes she had put big green bows.

'I reckon I'll be the finest lady at this party,' she muttered contentedly to herself as she rang the doorbell.

In the Settergrens' sitting room sat three very smart ladies, along with Tommy and Annika and their mother. There was a wonderful spread on the table and a fire was burning in the fireplace. The ladies chatted softly together while Tommy and Annika sat on the sofa looking at a photo album. It was all very peaceful.

But suddenly the peace was shattered.

'Preseeeeeent arms!'

A deafening shout came from the hall, and the next minute there stood Pippi Longstocking in the doorway. She had shouted so loudly and so unexpectedly that it had made the ladies almost jump off their chairs.

'Company quick MARCH!' they heard next, and Pippi strode briskly up to Mrs Settergren.

'Company HALT!' She stopped.

'Arms forward stretch, one TWO,' she yelled, and grasped Mrs Settergren's hand with both of her own and shook it vigorously.

'Knees BEND,' she shouted, and curtsied politely. Then she smiled at Mrs Settergren and said in her normal voice:

'I am actually quite shy, so if I don't take a firm grip of myself I would only stand in the hall making a fuss and not dare to come in.'

After which she charged up to the other ladies and kissed them on the cheek.

'Charmed, most charmed, I'm sure,' she said, because she had once heard a fine gentleman say that to a lady. Then she sat down on the best chair she could see. Mrs Settergren had thought the children could stay up in Tommy and Annika's room, but Pippi sat happily where she was, slapped her knees and said, looking at the table:

'That certainly looks very tasty. When do we start?'

Just then the family's home help, Ella, came in with the coffee pot, and Mrs Settergren said:

'Please help yourselves!'

'Me first!' yelled Pippi, and she was beside the table in two leaps. She grabbed as many cakes and biscuits as she could possibly fit on one plate, threw five sugar cubes into a coffee cup, emptied half the cream jug into it and returned to her chair before the ladies even had time to get to the table.

Pippi stretched out her legs in front of her and placed the plate on the tips of her toes. Then she dunked the biscuits happily into her coffee cup and crammed so many into her mouth in one go that she couldn't say a word, however hard she tried. In a trice she had finished everything on her plate. She stood up, banged on the plate as if it was a tambourine, and walked over to the table to see if there were any cakes or biscuits left. The ladies looked at her disapprovingly, but she didn't notice. Chatting merrily, she walked round the table, grabbing a cake here and a biscuit there.

'It was ever so kind of you to invite me,' she said. 'I've never been to a coffee party before.'

There was a huge cream gateau on the table, topped with a red fruit jelly. Pippi stood with her hands behind her back and stared at it. Suddenly she bent forwards and snatched the jelly between her teeth. But she dived in a little too fast because when she came up again her whole face was plastered in cream.

'Hahaha,' laughed Pippi. 'Now we can play blind man's buff because we've already got the blind man. I can't see a thing.'

She stuck out her tongue and licked off the cream.

'That was a terrible accident, wasn't it?' she said. 'But since the gateau is spoiled beyond repair I might as well eat it all up anyway.'

So she did. She attacked it with the cake slice and within a very short space of time the gateau had disappeared. Satisfied, Pippi patted her stomach. Mrs Settergren had been in the kitchen while this was going on and had no idea about the accident with the gateau. But the other ladies were looking at Pippi very sternly. They would probably have liked a piece of cake too. Pippi noticed they were looking unhappy and she decided to try and cheer them up.

'Don't be upset over such a little accident', she said, comfortingly. 'The main thing is we have our health. And a coffee party is supposed to be fun.'

She picked up the sugar bowl and scattered the

sugar cubes all over the carpet.

'Oh no, what's this?' she shrieked. 'How could I have made such a mistake? I thought it was the other kind of sugar, the kind you sprinkle over everything. But done is done.'

Then she took the sugar shaker which was standing on the table and scattered quite a lot of sugar all over the floor.

'Take note,' she said. 'This *is* sprinkly sugar, so I am perfectly entitled. What have we got sprinkly sugar for if not to sprinkle it, I'd like to know.'

'Have you noticed how nice it is to walk on a floor covered in sugar?' she asked the ladies. 'Even more fun in your bare feet, of course,' she continued, and pulled off her shoes and stockings. 'I think you ought to try it too. There's nothing nicer, believe me.'

Just then Mrs Settergren came in, and when she saw the spilled sugar on the floor she took a firm grip of Pippi's arm and led her over to Tommy and Annika on the sofa. Then she went and sat with the ladies and offered them a second cup of coffee. When she saw the gateau had gone she was extremely pleased. She thought her guests had liked it so much they had eaten it all up.

Pippi, Tommy, and Annika chatted quietly on the sofa. The fire crackled in the grate. The ladies drank their coffee and all was calm and peaceful again. And as sometimes happens at coffee parties, the ladies began discussing their home helps. The home helps they had found were not especially good, by the sound of it, because the ladies weren't satisfied with them at all, and they all agreed that in fact they shouldn't have home helps at all. It was better to do all the work yourself, because then at least you knew it was done properly.

Pippi sat on the sofa, listening, and when the ladies had talked about it for some time she said:

'My granny had a home help once called Malin. She had chilblains on her feet, but otherwise there was nothing wrong with her. The only bad thing about her was that as soon as they had visitors she ran up and bit them on the leg. And barked! Oh, how she barked! You could hear it all down the road. But she was only being playful. Not that the guests understood that. An old priest's wife came to visit Granny once when Malin was quite new, and when Malin came running up and set her teeth into the old woman's leg, the woman gave such a howl that it scared Malin so much she bit even harder. And then she couldn't let go. She was stuck to the old lady all week until Friday. So Granny had to peel her own potatoes that day. But then they were done properly, of course. She was so good at peeling that when she was finished there was no potato left at all. Only peel! But after that Friday the priest's wife didn't come to visit Granny again. She couldn't take a joke. And Malin was only being playful and enjoying herself! Though saying that, she could be easily offended too, there's no denying it. Once, when Granny stuck a fork in her ear, she sulked all day.' Pippi looked around, smiling cheerfully.

'Well, so much for Malin,' she said, rolling her thumbs.

The ladies looked as if they hadn't heard and they carried on talking.

'If only my Rosa kept herself clean,' said Mrs Berggren. 'Then I might possibly keep her. But she is as filthy as a pig.'

'Then you should have seen Malin,' Pippi chimed in. 'Malin was so whoppingly filthy that it was a joy to see, Granny always said. Once, at a bazaar in the City Hotel, she won first prize for the dirt under her nails. Mercy on us, how disgustingly grubby that woman was,' Pippi said joyfully.

Mrs Settergren threw her a stern look.

'Can you imagine,' said Mrs Granberg. 'The other evening, when my Britta was going out, she borrowed my blue silk dress, entirely without my permission. I mean, isn't that just about the last straw?'

'Oh, indeed,' said Pippi. 'She and Malin are alike as two peas in a pod, from what I hear. Granny had a pink woolly vest she was immensely fond of. But the worst thing was, Malin liked it too. And every morning Granny and Malin squabbled over who would wear the vest. Finally, they agreed to take turns every day, to make it fair. But oh, that Malin was nothing but trouble, I can tell you! Sometimes she would come running in when it wasn't even her turn and say: "There'll be no mashed turnip today unless I get the pink vest!" Well, what was Granny to do? Mashed turnip was her favourite food. There was nothing for it but to give Malin the vest! And when at last she got it, she went into the kitchen as nice as you like and mashed the turnip until it flew all over the walls.'

There was a short silence. But then Mrs Alexandersson said:

'I'm not entirely certain, but I strongly suspect that my Hulda steals things. I have actually noticed that things are going missing.'

'Malin—' began Pippi, but Mrs Settergren said firmly:

'Children, up to your room this minute!'

'Yes, but, I was only going to say that Malin stole things too,' said Pippi. 'Like a magpie! Left, right, and centre! She used to get up in the middle of the night and do some stealing, because otherwise she couldn't sleep, she said. Once she pinched Granny's piano and rammed it into her top drawer. She had very sticky fingers, Granny said.'

Tommy and Annika hooked their arms under Pippi's and dragged her upstairs. The ladies drank a third cup of coffee, and Mrs Settergren said:

'Not that I like to complain about my Ella, but she does break a lot of china, she really does.'

A red head appeared at the top of the stairs.

'Talking about Malin,' said Pippi. 'You might be wondering whether she used to break a lot of china. I should say so! She had a particular day for breaking the china. Tuesdays, Granny told me. As early as five in the morning you could hear that strapping girl down in the kitchen, smashing china. She would start with the coffee cups and a few small things, then move on to the pudding bowls and then the big flat plates, and finish with the serving dishes and soup tureens. There was such a crashing in the kitchen all morning it was a joy to hear, Granny said. And if Malin had any spare time in the afternoon she would go into the sitting room with a little hammer and wallop the antique East India plates that hung on the walls. Granny bought new china every Wednesday,' Pippi finished, and disappeared upstairs like a jack-in-the-box.

By now Mrs Settergren's patience had come to an end. She ran up the stairs, into the children's room and walked over to Pippi, who had just begun to teach Tommy to stand on his head.

'You're not allowed to come here ever again,' said Mrs Settergren. 'Because you behave so badly.'

Pippi looked at her in astonishment and then her eyes slowly filled with tears.

'I might have known I couldn't behave,' she said. 'There's no point even trying. I can never learn anyway. I should have stayed at sea.'

Then she gave Mrs Settergren a curtsy, said goodbye to Tommy and Annika, and went slowly down the stairs.

By now the ladies were also getting ready to go home. Pippi sat on the boot shelf in the hall and looked at the ladies as they put on their hats and coats.

'Such a pity you don't like your home helps,' she said. 'You should have one like Malin! You won't find a better maid, Granny always said. Do you know, one Christmas, when Malin was going to serve a roast piglet, do you know what she did? She'd read in a cookery book that roast piglet should be served with pleated paper in the ears and an apple in the mouth. Poor Malin didn't understand it was the piglet they were talking about. You should have seen her when she came in on Christmas Eve, wearing her apron and with a huge apple stuck in her mouth! Granny said to her: "What a nincompoop you are, Malin!" And of course Malin couldn't get out a word to defend herself but could only waggle her ears, which made the paper rustle. She tried to say something, but all that came out was "blubb, blubb, blubb." And of course, she couldn't bite people on the leg like she usually did, even though there were lots of visitors that day. No, it wasn't a happy

Christmas Eve for little Malin,' Pippi said glumly.

The ladies had their coats on by now and were saying their last goodbyes to Mrs Settergren. Pippi ran up to her and whispered:

'I'm sorry I couldn't behave! Cheerio!'

Then she flung on her big hat and went out with the ladies. Outside the gate they went different ways, Pippi to Villa Villekulla and the ladies in the opposite direction.

But they had only walked a short distance when they heard panting. It was Pippi running up behind them.

'You won't believe how sad Granny was to lose Malin. You see, one Tuesday morning, Malin hardly had time to break more than a dozen teacups before she ran off to sea. Granny had to smash the china herself that day. She wasn't used to it, poor thing, and it gave her blisters. After that she never saw Malin again. Such a waste of a first-rate maid, Granny said.'

Then Pippi left and the ladies hurried on their way. But they hadn't walked far before they heard her in the distance, yelling at the top of her lungs:

'T-h-a-t M-a-l-i-n, s-h-e n-e-v-e-r s-w-e-p-t u-n-d-e-r t-h-e b-e-d-s!'

PIPPI BECOMES
A LIFESAVER

One Sunday afternoon Pippi was thinking what to do. Tommy and Annika and their mum and dad had been invited out to tea, so she couldn't expect a visit from them.

The day had been full of nice activities. She had got up early and taken Mr Nilsson orange squash and buns in bed. He looked so sweet sitting there in his light blue nightshirt, holding the glass in both hands. Then she had fed and brushed the horse and told him a long story about her adventures at sea. After that she had gone into the sitting room and painted an enormous picture on the wallpaper. It was a picture of a rather large lady in a red dress and black hat. In one hand she was holding a flower and in the other a dead rat. It was a very beautiful painting, thought Pippi. It brightened up the whole room. After that she had sat at her writing bureau looking at all her birds' eggs and shells, and that made her think of all the places where she and her dad had collected them, and all the nice little shops all over the world where they had bought the precious things she kept in the bureau drawers. Then she had tried to teach Mr Nilsson to dance the polka, but he didn't want to. For one moment she had considered trying to teach the horse, but for some reason she crawled inside the log box instead and shut the lid. She played at being a sardine in a sardine tin, but it wasn't much fun without Tommy and Annika being there and pretending to be sardines as well.

But now it was beginning to get dark. She pressed her little potato-nose up against the window and looked out at the chilly autumn evening. Then she remembered that she hadn't been out riding for a few days, so she decided to do that right away. It would be a nice end to a pleasant Sunday.

So she went and put on her big hat, fetched Mr Nilsson, who was sitting in a corner playing with some marbles, saddled her horse and lifted him down from the veranda. And off they set, Mr Nilsson on Pippi, and Pippi on the horse.

It was quite cold and the roads were icy, and there was a lot of crunching and cracking as they galloped along. Mr Nilsson sat on Pippi's shoulder and tried to grab some of the branches of the trees, but Pippi was riding too fast. On the other hand, he received more than a few slaps around the ears from the branches as they passed, and it was hard for him to keep his straw hat on his head.

Pippi rode through the little town and people anxiously backed up against the buildings as she stormed past.

Naturally, the little town had a square with a small yellow-painted town hall alongside a few beautiful old buildings, all of them only one floor high. There was an ugly great building there too, newly-built and with three floors, known as the Skyscraper because it was taller than all the other buildings in the town.

At this time on a Sunday evening the little town seemed very quiet and peaceful. But suddenly the calm was broken by a loud shout:

'The Skyscraper's burning! Fire! Fire!'

From every direction people came running, wide-eyed. A fire engine drove through the streets with its siren blaring, and all the small children who otherwise thought it was fun to see a fire engine now cried in fright because they thought their homes would catch fire too. The square below the Skyscraper was crammed full of people and the police were trying to hold them back to let the fire engine through. Tongues of flame burst from the Skyscraper's windows, and smoke and sparks enveloped the firefighters who bravely tried to put out the fire.

The fire had started on the ground floor but quickly spread to the floors above. Suddenly the onlookers in the square saw a sight that made them gasp in horror. At the very top of the building was an attic window, and in the window that had just been opened by a tiny hand stood two little boys, crying out for help.

'We can't get out because someone has set fire to the stairs,' shouted the bigger of the two boys.

He was five years old and his brother was one year younger. Their mother had popped out on an errand and here they were, all alone. Many people down below began to cry, and the fire chief looked worried. There was a ladder on the fire engine, naturally, but it wasn't nearly long enough. Going into the building to bring out the boys was impossible. A great feeling of despair settled over the people watching from the square when they realized that nothing could be done to help the children. And the poor little boys stood there in the window, crying. It would only be a few minutes before the fire reached the attic.

Among the people watching was Pippi on her horse. She looked at the fire engine with interest and was thinking about buying one for herself. She liked it because it was red and because it had made so much noise as it sped through the streets. Then she looked at the crackling fire and she liked the way the sparks dropped all around her.

Eventually she noticed the little boys at the attic window. To her surprise they didn't seem to be finding the fire especially exciting. She couldn't understand that at all, until she asked the people around her:

'Why are the boys screaming?'

At first she heard only sobs in reply, but then a fat gent said to her:

'Well, why do you think? Don't you think you'd

be screaming too if you were trapped up there and couldn't get down?'

'I never scream,' said Pippi. 'But if they want to get down why isn't anyone helping them?'

'Because they can't, of course,' said the fat gent.

Pippi thought about that for a while.

'Can someone fetch a long rope?' she asked.

'What's the point of that?' replied the fat gent. 'The boys are too young to climb down a rope. And anyway, how would you be able to get a rope up to them?'

'Oh, I've done a bit of sailing in my time,' Pippi said calmly. 'I want a rope.'

No one thought it would do any good, but somehow a rope was found for Pippi.

At one end of the Skyscraper was a tall tree and the top of the tree was more or less the same height as the attic window. But between the tree and the window was a gap of at least three metres. And the tree trunk was bare, with no branches to stand on. Even Pippi wouldn't be able to climb up there.

The fire raged, the boys at the window screamed and all the people in the town square cried.

Pippi got down from the horse and walked over to the tree. Then she took the rope and tied it round Mr Nilsson's tail.

'Now you must be a good boy for Pippi,' she told him. She put him on the tree trunk and gave him a little push. He knew very well what he had to do and he climbed obediently up the tree. For a little monkey it wasn't hard to do.

Everyone in the square held their breath and watched Mr Nilsson. Soon he reached the top of the tree and there he sat on a branch, looking down at Pippi. She beckoned to him to come down again. He did, but this time on the other side of the branch, so that when Mr Nilsson reached the ground again the rope was looped over the branch and was now hanging double with both ends on the ground.

'You know, Mr Nilsson, you are so wise you could be a professor any time you like,' said Pippi, and untied the knot that was holding the end of the rope to Mr Nilsson's tail.

Close by was a building that was being repaired. Pippi ran over and found a long plank. She put it under her arm, ran back to the tree, grabbed hold of the rope with her free hand and put her feet against the tree trunk. Swiftly and nimbly she climbed the trunk, and everyone stopped

crying from utter amazement. When she reached the top she rested the plank on a thick branch and carefully pushed one end towards the attic window. And there it lay, like a bridge between the tree and the window.

The people watching down below stood in absolute silence. They couldn't speak because they were so tense. Pippi stepped out onto the plank. She smiled kindly at both the boys in the window.

'You look very sad,' she said. 'Have you got a tummy ache?'

She ran across the plank and jumped in through the window.

'It feels a bit hot in here,' she said. 'You won't need to heat the room today, I guarantee you that. And only four logs at the very most tomorrow, I would imagine.'

She picked up a boy under each arm and stepped back onto the plank.

'Now you're going to have a bit of fun at last,' she said. 'This is almost like walking on a tightrope.'

And when she reached the middle of the plank she balanced on one leg, just as she had done at the circus. Then a murmur ran through the crowd in the square below, and when shortly afterwards Pippi lost one shoe several elderly ladies fainted. But Pippi and the boys reached the other side safe and sound and everyone applauded so loudly it rang through the dark evening and drowned out the roar of the fire.

Pippi hauled up the rope and tied one end firmly to a branch. Then she tied one of the boys to the other end and let him sail slowly down to his overjoyed mother waiting below. She threw herself over her boy and hugged him with tears in her eyes. But Pippi called out:

'Come on, untie the rope! There's another kid up here and he can't fly either.'

So people helped to undo the knot and set the boy free. Pippi was certainly very good at tying knots! Then she hauled up the rope again and now it was the other boy's turn to be lowered down.

Now only Pippi was left in the tree. She ran out onto the plank and everyone watched her, wondering what she was going to do. Pippi danced up and down on the narrow plank. She waved her arms about so elegantly and sang in a croaky voice which could just about be heard by the folk below:

'A fire is burning,
Burning so bright,
It's probably scaring my horse.
It's burning for you,
It's burning for me,
And for all of us dancing the waltz.'

As she sang she danced more and more wildly and many people in the square shut their eyes in fear because they thought she would fall off and plunge to her death. Long flames shot out through the attic window and in the glow they could see Pippi very clearly. She lifted her arms to the evening sky and as a shower of sparks rained down over her she shrieked:

'Oh, what a wonderful, wonderful blaze!'

Then she leaped onto the rope.

'Yippee!' she whooped, and shot to the ground like greased lightning.

'Three cheers for Pippi Longstocking!' shouted the fire chief.

'Hooray, hooray, hooray!' yelled all the people. But someone yelled it four times. And that someone was Pippi.

PIPPI CELEBRATES
HER BIRTHDAY

One day Tommy and Annika found a letter in their letter box.

TO TMMY AND ANIKER it said on the outside. And when they opened it, this is what it said:

TMMY AND ANIKER MUST KOME TO PIPPIS

BERTHDAY PARTY TOMMORO AFTANOON. DRESS:

WARE WOT YOU FEEL LIKE.

Tommy and Annika were so happy that they started leaping and dancing about. They could read exactly what the letter said, even though the spelling was a little strange. Pippi had found it terribly hard to write. Naturally, she knew the letter 'i' from that day in school, but the truth was, she actually could do some writing. During the time she was sailing the ocean, one of the sailors on her dad's boat used to sit with her on the quarterdeck in the evenings, trying to teach her to write. Unfortunately, Pippi wasn't a child who could concentrate for long. All of a sudden she would say:

'Tell you what, Fridolf,' (that was the sailor's name) 'I don't give two hoots about this reading lark. I'm off up the mast to see what the weather will be like tomorrow.'

That's why it wasn't strange that she found writing hard. It took a whole night for her to write out that invitation and towards dawn, when the stars were fading above Villa Villekulla's roof, she tiptoed over to Tommy and Annika's house and put the letter in their letter box.

As soon as Tommy and Annika came home from school they started smartening themselves up for Pippi's party. Annika asked her mum if she would curl her hair, so that's what her mum did. She also tied a wide, pink, silk ribbon in Annika's hair. Tommy combed his hair with water to make it really flat and shiny. He definitely didn't want to be curly. Annika wanted to put on her very best frock but her mum said it wasn't worth it, because

Annika rarely came home clean and tidy from Pippi's house. So Annika had to content herself with her second-best frock. Tommy really didn't mind what he put on as long as he was looking more or less smart.

They had a present for Pippi, of course. They had taken money from their own piggy banks and on the way home from school they had run into the toyshop on Storgatan and bought a really lovely . . . well, that will have to be a secret for the time being. For now the present was wrapped in green paper with lots of ribbon, and when Tommy and Annika were ready Tommy carried the present and they trotted off, followed by their mum's anxious instructions to look after their clothes. Annika was also going to carry the present some of the way, and when they handed it over they would both be holding it, so they agreed.

♥

It was now November and sunset came early. When Tommy and Annika walked through Pippi's gate they held each other's hand tightly because it was dark in Pippi's garden, and the old trees that were losing the last of their leaves were whispering mournfully.

'Very autumnal,' said Tommy.

That's why it was so nice to see all the windows lit up in Villa Villekulla and know they were going there for a birthday party.

Usually Tommy and Annika went in through the kitchen entrance, but today they chose the front door. There was no sign of the horse on the veranda. Tommy knocked on the door politely. From inside they heard a muffled voice:

'Who is it on this dark, dark night,

Coming to my house?

Is it a ghost, or could it be

A lonely little mouse?'

'No, Pippi, it's us!' Annika cried. 'Open the door!'

And Pippi opened the door.

'Oh, Pippi, why did you say that about a ghost? I got so scared,' Annika said, completely forgetting to wish Pippi a happy birthday.

Pippi laughed cheerfully and threw open the kitchen door. Oh, how lovely it was to come into the light and the warmth! The birthday party was going to be in the kitchen because it was cosiest in there.

There were only two other rooms on the

ground floor. One was the sitting room with one piece of furniture inside, and the other was Pippi's bedroom. But the kitchen was big and roomy, and Pippi had made it look neat and tidy. On the floor she had laid out mats and on the table was a new tablecloth Pippi had made. The flowers she had embroidered looked a little odd, it's true, but Pippi assured them that such flowers grew in Farthest India, so all was as it should be. The curtains were closed and a lively fire was crackling in the fireplace. Mr Nilsson was sitting on the log box banging two saucepan lids together, and in a far corner stood the horse. Naturally, he was also invited to the party.

At last Tommy and Annika remembered to wish Pippi a happy birthday. Tommy bowed and Annika made a curtsy, and they handed over the green parcel and said:

'Congratulations on your birthday.'

Pippi thanked them and ripped off the paper enthusiastically. Inside was a tin music box! Pippi was wild with joy. She patted Tommy and she patted Annika and she patted the music box and she patted the wrapping paper. Then she turned the handle of the music box and with a lot of plinging and plonging out came a tune that was meant to be *Oh, my darling Clementine.*

Pippi turned the handle round and round and seemed to forget everything else. Then suddenly she remembered something.

'My giddy aunt, you must have your birthday presents too!'

'But it isn't our birthdays,' Tommy said.

Pippi looked at them, astounded.

'No, but it's my birthday, isn't it? That means I can give you birthday presents. Or is it written somewhere in your school books that you can't do that? Has it got something to do with multikipperation that makes it not allowed?'

'No, of course it's allowed,' Tommy said. 'Though it's not usual. As far as I'm concerned I'd love to have a present.'

'Me too,' said Annika.

Then Pippi ran into the sitting room and fetched two parcels that were standing on the writing bureau. When Tommy opened his parcel he found a kind of small ivory flute, and in Annika's parcel was a beautiful brooch in the shape of a butterfly. The butterfly's wings were inset with red, blue and green jewels.

Now that everyone had been given their birthday presents it was time to eat. There were piles of cakes and biscuits on the table. The biscuits were funny shapes, but Pippi insisted they were the kind people ate in China.

Then Pippi poured hot chocolate into mugs and topped it with whipped cream, and they could all sit down. But first Tommy said:

'When Mum and Dad have guests for dinner the men always get a card telling them the name of the lady they must escort to the table. I think we ought to do that.'

'Fire away,' said Pippi.

'Although it's harder for us because I'm the only man,' Tommy said, uncertainly.

'That's news to me,' Pippi said. 'Do you think Mr Nilsson is a woman?'

'No, no, of course not. I forgot Mr Nilsson,' said Tommy. And he sat down on the log box and wrote a card:

Mr Settergren has the pleasure of escorting Miss Longstocking.

'Mr Settergren, that's me,' he said proudly, as he showed Pippi the card. Then he wrote the next card:

Mr Nilsson has the pleasure of escorting Miss Settergren.

'The horse must have a card as well,' said Pippi firmly. 'Even if he isn't sitting at the table!'

So on Pippi's instructions Tommy wrote the following:

The horse has the pleasure of staying in the corner where he will be served biscuits and sugar.

Pippi held the card under the horse's nose and said:

'Read this and tell me what you think!'

And since the horse didn't have any objections, Tommy led Pippi to sit at the table. Mr Nilsson made no attempt to lead Annika, so Annika quite simply picked him up and carried him to the table. He refused to sit on a chair, however, but sat directly on the table. He didn't want hot chocolate with whipped cream either, but when Pippi poured water in his cup he seized it with both hands and drank.

Annika, Tommy and Pippi tucked in and enjoyed the food, and Annika said that if these were the biscuits they ate in China she would move there when she was grown up.

When Mr Nilsson had emptied his cup he

turned it upside down and put it on his head. When Pippi saw that, she did the same, but because she hadn't drunk all the chocolate a little stream started running down her forehead and over her nose. Pippi stuck out her tongue and stopped it.

'Waste not, want not,' she said.

Tommy and Annika licked their cups clean before putting them on their heads.

When they were all full up and happy, and the horse had been given his food, Pippi took a firm grip of the four corners of the tablecloth and lifted it up so that all the cups and plates tumbled on top of each other as if they were in a sack. Then she stuffed the whole bundle into the wood box.

'I always like to get the clearing up done as soon as I've eaten,' she said.

Then it was time for games. Pippi suggested they play one called Don't Touch the Floor. It was very simple. All they had to do was make their way round the kitchen without putting a single foot on the floor. Pippi scuttled round in a flash, but Tommy and Annika did quite well too. They started on the draining board and if they stretched out their legs as far as they could they could get to the stove, then from the stove to the log box, the log box to the hat rack, down on to the table and from there over two stools to the corner cupboard. Between the corner cupboard and the draining board there was a distance of several metres, but luckily that's where the horse was standing and if they climbed onto his back at the tail end and slid along to his head end, and just at the right moment made a jump for it, they would land on the draining board.

When they had been playing this for a while and Annika's dress was no longer her second-best but her next to, next to, next to second-best, and Tommy was as dirty as a chimney sweep, they decided to think up another game.

'What about going up to the attic and saying hello to the ghosts?' Pippi suggested.

Annika gasped.

'Are . . . are . . . there ghosts in the attic?' she asked.

'I should say so! Masses!' replied Pippi. 'It's knee-deep in all kinds of ghosts and spooky things up there. You can't move without tripping over them.'

'Oh,' said Annika, looking at Pippi and frowning.

'Mum says there's no such thing as ghosts and ghouls,' Tommy said confidently.

'Too true,' said Pippi. 'Nowhere else but here, because all of them live in my attic and it's a waste of time asking them to move. But they're not dangerous. They only pinch your arm and give you bruises, and they howl. And they practise bowling using their heads.'

'Pr . . . pr . . . practise bowling using their heads?' whispered Annika.

'That's exactly what they do,' said Pippi. 'Come on, let's go up and have a chat with them. I'm tip-top at bowling.'

Tommy didn't want to let on that he was afraid, and in a kind of way he really did want to see a ghost. It would be something to tell the boys at school. And he comforted himself by thinking the ghosts wouldn't dare tackle Pippi. He decided to go with her. Poor Annika, nothing would persuade her to go, but then she imagined a little ghost gliding down to her in the kitchen while she was sitting there all alone.

That did it! Better to be with Pippi and Tommy among a thousand ghosts than on her own with even the tiniest little baby ghost in the kitchen!

Pippi went first. She opened the door to the attic stairs. It was as black as night. Tommy held tightly onto Pippi, and Annika held Tommy even tighter. They went up the stairs, which creaked and groaned with every step they took. Tommy started to wonder if it would have been better not to go, but Annika didn't need to wonder. She was convinced of it.

Eventually the stairs came to an end and they were standing in the attic. It was completely dark apart from a thin strip of moonlight that fell across the floor. Sighing and whistling came from every corner as the wind blew in through the cracks.

'Hello, all you ghosts!' called Pippi.

But if there was a ghost there, he didn't answer.

'I might have known,' said Pippi. 'They've gone to a meeting of the Spook and Ghost Society.'

Annika gave a sigh of relief and she hoped the meeting would last for a very long time. But at that very moment an awful sound came from a far corner of the attic.

'Clewwiitt,' it said, and a moment later Tommy saw something come swooshing towards him in the dim light. He felt a gust of wind against his forehead and saw something black disappear through a tiny window that was open. He screamed his head off.

'A ghost! A ghost!'

And Annika joined in.

'The poor thing will arrive too late for the meeting,' said Pippi. 'If it was a ghost, that is. And not an owl! By the way, there aren't any ghosts,' she went on after a moment. 'So the more I think of it, the more it was an owl. If anyone suggests ghosts exist, I'll twist their nose off.'

'Yes, but, you said so yourself,' said Annika.

'What? Did I?' Pippi said. 'Then I'll most definitely twist my nose off.' And she took a firm grasp of her nose and twisted it.

After this, Tommy and Annika felt a little calmer. They were even brave enough to walk to the window and look out over the garden. Big, dark clouds scudded across the sky and did their best to hide the moon, and the trees sighed.

Tommy and Annika turned round. But then— horror of horrors—a white figure was coming towards them.

'A ghost!' screamed Tommy in a panic.

Annika was so afraid she couldn't even scream.

The figure came closer and closer, and Tommy and Annika clung onto each other and shut their eyes. But then they heard the ghost say:

'Look what I found! Dad's old nightshirt, in that seaman's chest over there. If I sew it up to about here I can actually use it myself.'

Pippi walked up to them with the nightshirt flapping around her legs.

'Oh, Pippi, I almost died of fright,' Annika said.

'But nightshirts aren't dangerous,' Pippi declared. 'They only bite in self-defence.'

Pippi then decided to have a thorough search of the seaman's chest. She carried it over to the window and threw open the lid. The faint moonlight fell over the contents. Inside lay heaps of old clothes that she pulled out and dropped on the attic floor. There was also a telescope, a couple of old books, three pistols, a sword, and a bag of golden coins.

'Diddly-oh and diddly-eye,' said Pippi happily.

'How exciting!' Tommy said.

Pippi gathered everything up in the nightshirt and down they went to the kitchen again. Annika was very pleased to leave the attic.

'Never let children play with weapons,' Pippi

said, taking a pistol in each hand. 'Otherwise there could easily be an accident,' she continued, pressing the trigger of both pistols at the same time. 'They went off very nicely,' she said, and looked up at the ceiling. There were two holes where the bullets had gone in.

'Who knows?' she said, sounding optimistic. 'Maybe the bullets have gone right through the ceiling and hit a ghost in the leg. That'll give them something to think about next time they decide to scare small innocent children. Because even if they don't exist, there's still no reason to scare the wits out of people. Would you like a pistol each, by the way?' she asked.

Tommy was thrilled and Annika really wanted a pistol too, so long as it wasn't loaded.

'Now we can build our own band of robbers if we want,' said Pippi, and put the telescope to her eye. 'I can practically see the fleas in South America with this, I think,' she carried on. 'This will be very useful too, if we're going to be a band of robbers.'

Just then there was a knock on the door. It was Tommy and Annika's dad come to fetch his children home. It was long past their bedtime, he said. Tommy and Annika had to hurry to say thank you and goodbye and gather up all their belongings—the flute, the brooch and the pistols.

Pippi went with her guests to the veranda and watched them disappear down the garden path. They turned around and waved at her. She was caught in the light from inside. There she stood with her red plaits sticking out and her father's nightshirt flapping around her feet. In one hand she held the pistol and in the other the sword, thrusting it about.

As Tommy and Annika and their father reached the gate, they heard her call something to them. They stopped and listened. The wind was blowing in the trees so they could hardly hear her. But they did hear.

'I'm going to be a pirate when I grow up,' she called. 'Are *you*?'

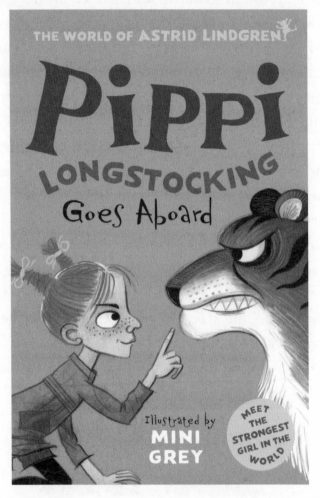

Pippi is back and as crazy and as funny as ever! But for Tommy and Annika, the fun might stop all too soon if Pippi agrees to go back to sea with her father.

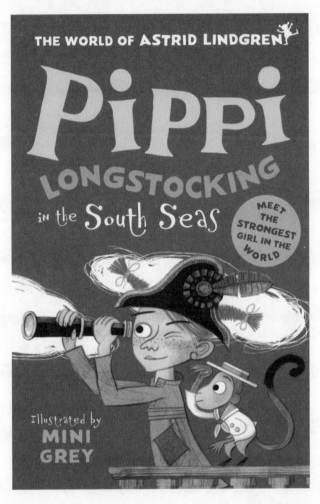

Pippi, Tommy and Annika go on their greatest adventure yet to Koratuttutt Island, where Pippi's father is king.

ABOUT THE AUTHOR

Astrid Lindgren was born in 1907, and grew up at a farm called Näs in the south of Sweden. Her first book was published in 1944, followed a year later by *Pippi Longstocking*. She wrote 34 chapter books and 41 picture books, that all together have sold 165 million copies worldwide. Her books have been translated into 107 different languages and according to UNESCO's annual list, she is the 18th most translated author in the world.

She created stories about Pippi, a free-spirited, red-haired girl, to entertain her daughter, Karin, who was ill with pneumonia. The girl's name 'Pippi Longstocking' was in fact invented by Karin. Astrid Lindgren once commented about her work, 'I write to amuse the child within me, and can only hope that other children may have some fun that way, too.'

For more information visit www.astridlindgren.com

THE WORLD OF
ASTRID LINDGREN

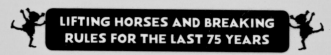

LIFTING HORSES AND BREAKING RULES FOR THE LAST 75 YEARS

Have you ever performed at the circus?

Pippi has!

Can you wiggle your toes while you're sleeping?

Pippi can!

Are you going to be a pirate when you grow up?

Pippi is!

Pippi lives in a house with a horse, a monkey, a suitcase full of gold, and no grown-ups to tell her what to do. She's wild and funny and her crazy ideas have a way of making *anything* exciting!

Other titles available in the series

OXFORD
UNIVERSITY PRESS

www.oup.com
www.oxfordowl.co.uk

ISBN 978-0-19-277631-0

9 780192 776310

£5.99 RRP

Julia Donaldson

Princess Mirror-Belle

illustrated by

Lydia Monks

218912 EN
Princess Mirror-Belle

Donaldson. Julia

ATOS BL: 4.9
Points: 2.0   LY